# THE GHOST SHIP

This edition first published in 2014 by Book House

© 2015 The Salariya Book Company Ltd

Distributed by Black Rabbit Books
P.O. Box 3263
Mankato
Minnesota MN 56002

First published in France by Éditions Flammarion MMVII

Copyright text and illustration © Éditions Flammarion MMVII

The right of Alain Surget to be identified as the author of this work and the
right of Annette Marnat to be identified as the illustrator of this work  has
been asserted in accordance with sections 77 and 78 of the Copyright, Designs
and Patents Act, 1988.

English edition © The Salariya Book Company
& Bailey Publishing Associates MMXI

Translated by Charlotte Coombe

Editor: Shirley Willis

Printed in the United States of America.
Printed on paper from sustainable forests.

Cataloging-in-Publication Data is available
from the Library of Congress

ISBN: 978-1-909645-41-7

The text for this book is set in 1Stone Serif
The display types are set in OldClaude

Written by
**Alain Surget**

Illustrated by
**Annette Marnat**

# THE GHOST
# SHIP

Translated by
Jill Lewin

# BOOK HOUSE

# Chapter I

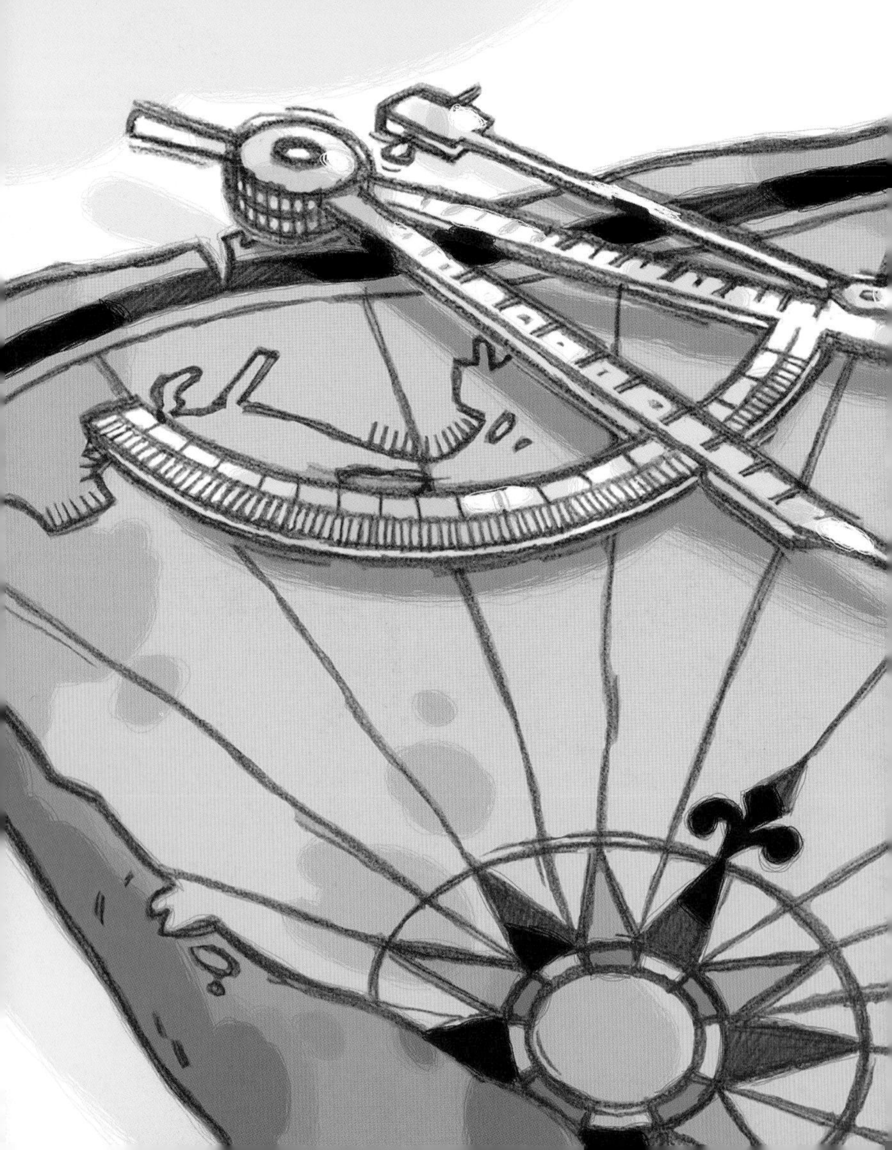

# A sailor’s life

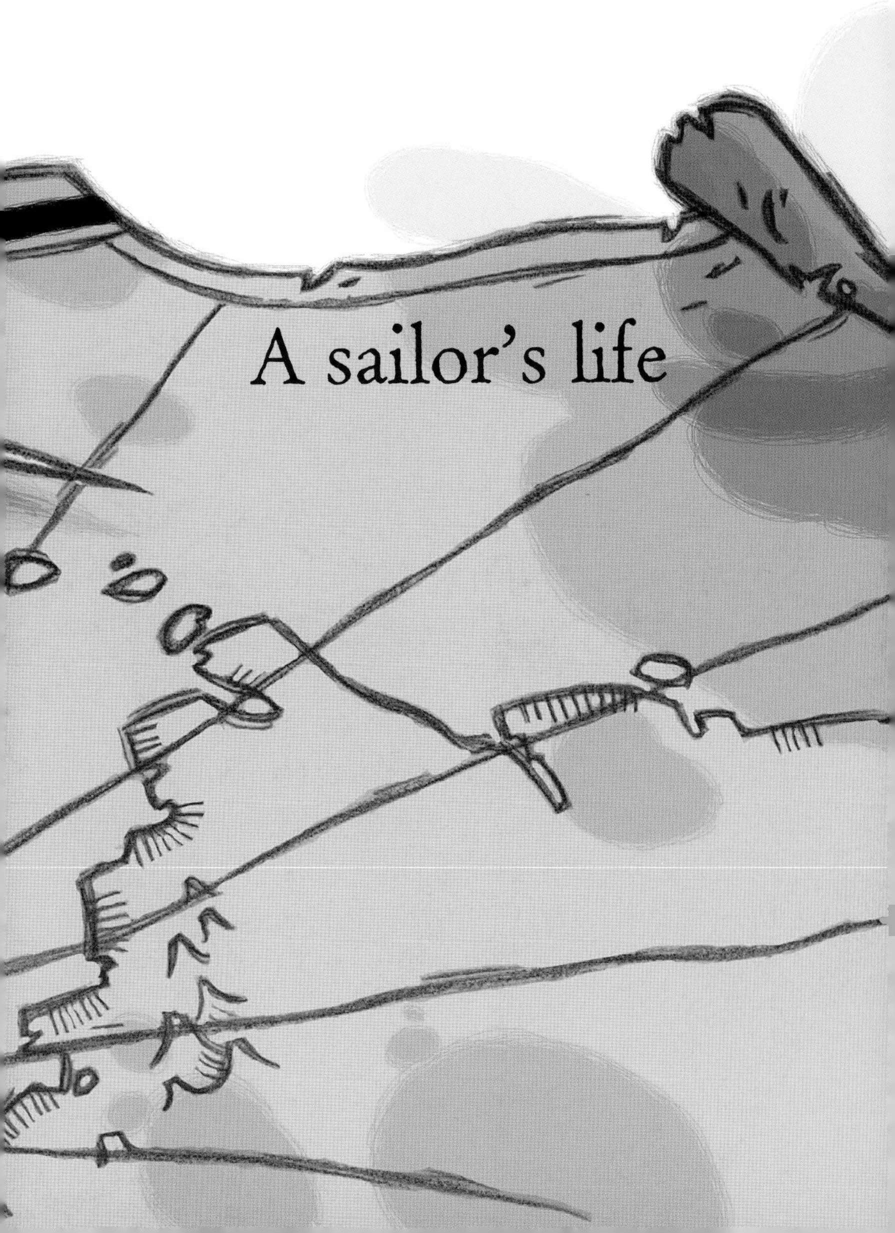

In full sail, the *Angry Flea* sped onward toward the New World, where—it was said—cities of gold still sparkled in the sunlight.

"This is where we are now…" said On-the-Fence, pointing. "And that's where we're heading!"

He ran his finger around the edges of an island on the map. Benjamin was sitting alongside him in the cabin with his elbows on the table. He was following the explanation carefully. On-the-Fence was second in command to the ship's captain, the Marquis de Parabas. Nicknamed On-the-Fence because he never answered a question with a straight "yes" or "no," he was showing the boy how to read a map.

"That's Hispaniola," said Benjamin. "That little

island to the North is Tortuga, and this one to the south is Île à Vache."

"You have a gift for this, my boy," On-the-Fence acknowledged in admiration. "I've never seen anyone learn so quickly!"

"I love studying. But not my sister... she prefers action. All she thinks about is fighting. Île à Vache is where our father's hiding!" Benjamin declared.

"Possibly," On-the-Fence replied. "In any case, that's where we're heading."

"Now, how do you know we're going in the right direction?"

"That's what the compass is for. The helmsman has one right in front of him that he uses to keep the ship on course. Let's go up on the poop deck," he suggested to Benjamin. "You can take the helm and see how the compass works."

They came out of the cabin. The sea was calm, but the sky wasn't as blue as it had been in the morning. A fine layer of mist softened the light, blurring the line of the horizon.

Some of the crew were on deck, checking that cannons were properly stowed and that the halyards were tight enough to hold the masts. Other members of the crew lounged against coils of rope, resting. Benjamin and On-the-Fence climbed up to the poop deck. There, they found Benjamin's sister, Louise. She had swapped her dress for men's clothing, and was practicing sword fighting with the captain, the mysterious Marquis de Parabas.

"You'll wear yourself out jumping around like that. You're spinning like a windmill. You need to be more supple," advised Parabas. "Your left leg needs to go back, bend your right leg, dodge my

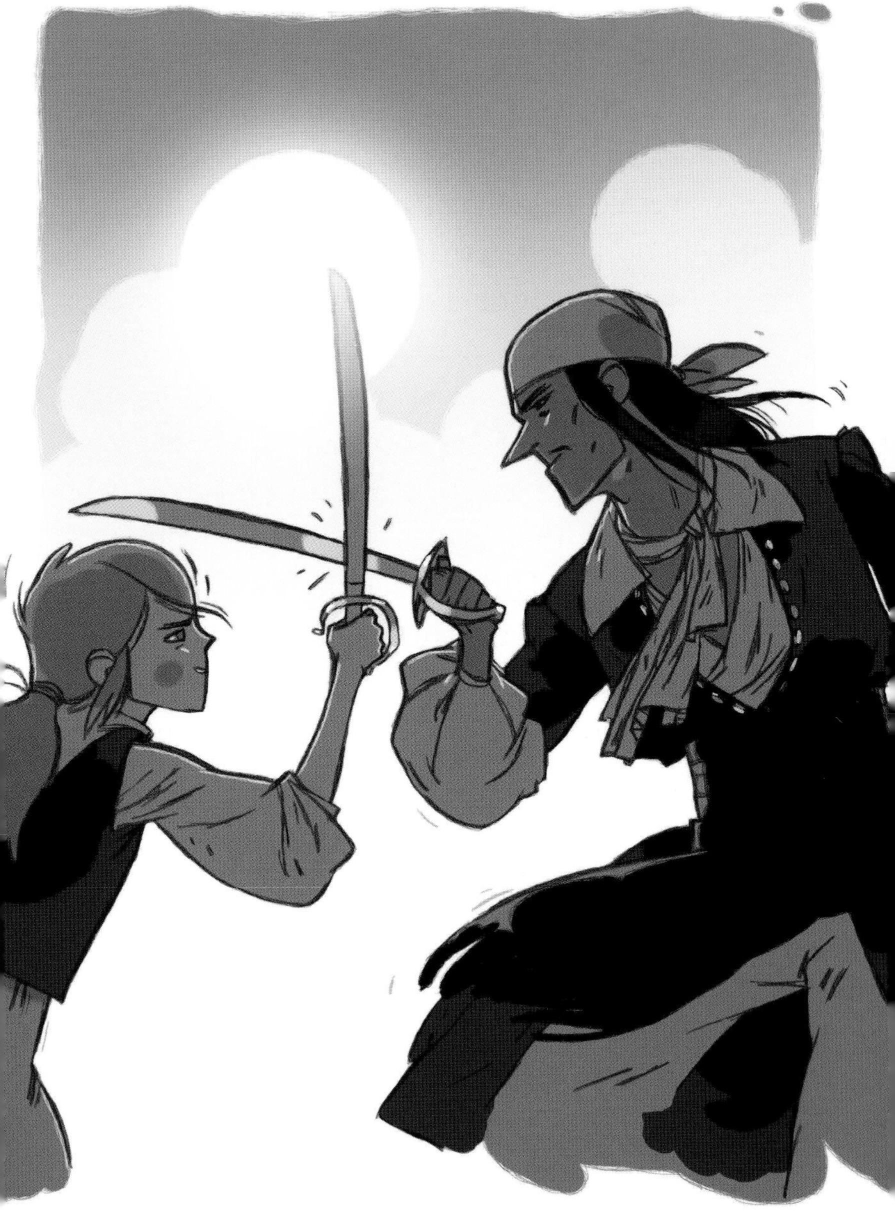

thrust… and lunge forward!"

Louise's blade plunged toward the marquis, but there was a "chink" as he parried it with a simple turn of his wrist. Louise's sword flew out of her hand and clattered down at the feet of the newcomers.

"Zerrro! Zerrro!" squawked Shut-your-trap! The gray parrot was perched nearby on a rope.

Louise stuck her tongue out at him and then went to pick up her sword. The helmsman made way for Benjamin and the boy took the wheel proudly. Swords continued to clash while Benjamin fixed his eyes on the compass housed in the binnacle.

"OK, that's enough for today!" Parabas declared after a little while. "It's time that you and your brother learned some of the crew's other tasks. The bosun will give you buckets and brushes, and you can scrub the decks!"

"What?" snorted Louise. "Get down on all fours and wear our knees out on those planks?"

"We're Cap'n Roc's children…" added Benjamin hopefully, "and he's one of the most famous pirates in the Carribean. We don't have to swab the deck like…"

Parabas called the bosun over and told him to equip the children for the job. But no sooner had he brought the brushes than Louise threw them into the sea.

"There!" she said defiantly. "Now how are we supposed to scrub the decks?"

The next moment, the twins found themselves on their knees, dipping their shirttails into the bucket. A group of sailors surrounded them, laughing.

"Keep your nerrrve!" commanded Shut-your-trap!. "Rrrub-a-dub-dub! Want it to sparrrkle! Son of a sharrrk!"

# Chapter II

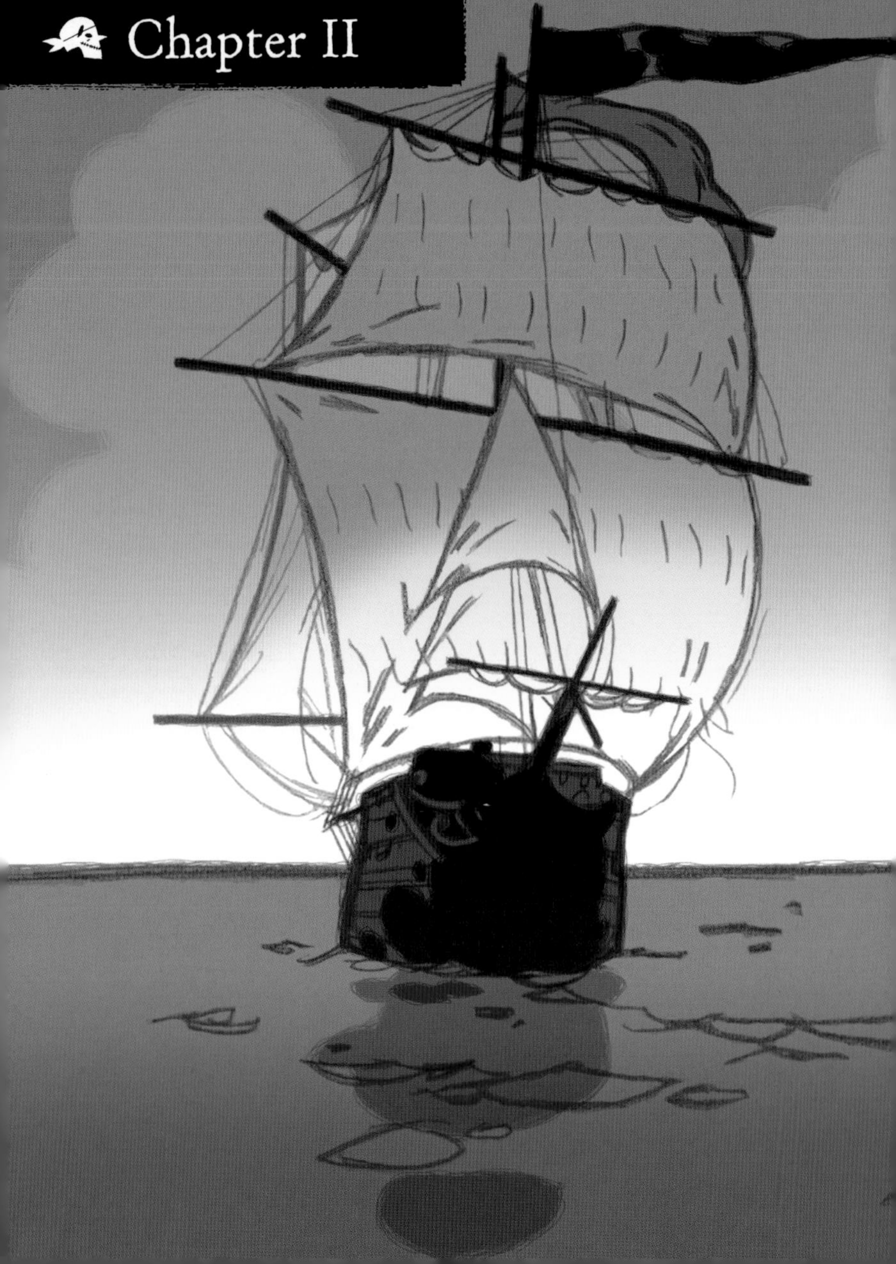

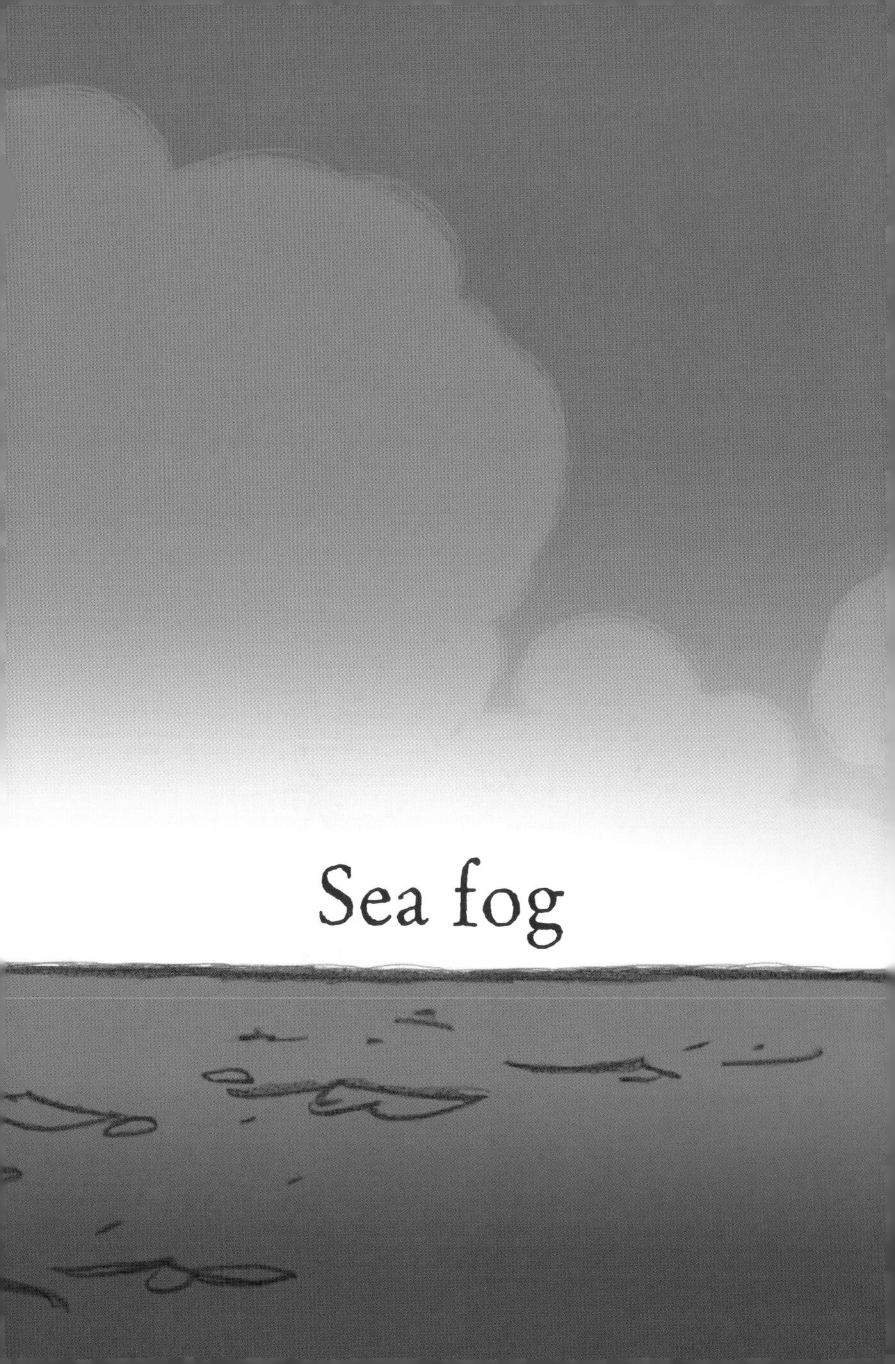

# Sea fog

The sky gradually took on a white, milky appearance and before long a dense fog had settled on the ocean. The thick, damp fog enveloped the *Angry Flea*, drenching her sails with tiny droplets of water. The men hurriedly lashed down the lanterns at the prow, the poop deck, the sides of the ship, and the tops of the masts.

"Hey, you two!" the bosun shouted urgently to the twins. "Drop your buckets! Go and get changed and climb up into the rigging with these horns. Blow on 'em until your lungs burst! We'll be done for in this pea-souper if a ship looms straight out of the fog at us!"

He handed a horn to each of them. The children quickly changed into dry shirts and then climbed reluctantly up through the ropes to the first "top"—a platform just under the lower sails.

"I feel as though I'm floating in the clouds," said Benjamin. "I can't even see the sea below us any more. You can only work out where the sun is from that brighter patch above us!"

The twins each put a horn to their lips and managed to get a loud drone from it. They sounded their horns to port and starboard and then straight ahead, as a warning of the *Angry Flea*'s path.

"We'll wake Neptune with this..." Benjamin began.

The rest of his sentence stuck in his throat. Was he seeing things? Two skeleton-like masts had just pierced through the fog, to starboard. That's all he could see. The black masts loomed out of the fog like crucifixes, so close that they seemed to be part of the *Angry Flea*.

"Lou... Louise! Look! Over there... a..." he stammered, grabbing her arm.

His sister, who had her back to him and was still blowing her horn, had seen nothing.

Then a shout went up from the deck, followed by cries of panic. The crew had seen the danger too.

"Hard to port!" yelled Parabas.

The helmsman pulled hard on the wheel, causing the ship to lurch so violently that it almost tore the mast away. The children instinctively crouched low in the rigging to avoid being thrown off the topmast.

They screamed as the ship threatened to capsize. The shape of a huge vessel suddenly loomed over them and its prow smashed into the *Angry Flea*. The impact wrenched the ropes from the twin's hands and sent them flying. With arms flailing, they tried to grasp hold of the ropes again but fell back into the halyards and disappeared from view.

The hulls of the two ships scraped together

noisily and then drifted apart. *The Angry Flea* bobbed up and down in the wake created by the impact, while the other ship floated off into the fog.

"It's the *Flying Dutchman*!" shouted the bosun. "I recognize its figurehead."

The *Flying Dutchman*! This was the infamous ghost ship that was doomed to sail the oceans for all eternity. The name sent a shudder through the crew.

"Let's get away quickly in case it drags us down in its wake," On-the-Fence yelled.

Having given the order to change course, Roger de Parabas raised his eyes to the mast and shouted:

"The kids! Where are the kids? I can't see them in the rigging! Let's hope they haven't fallen overboard... or worse, into the ghost ship!"

"Ghost ship? Arrrg..." screeched the parrot as he hid under Parabas' big hat.

"Come out of there," the captain ordered. "I've got a mission for you!"

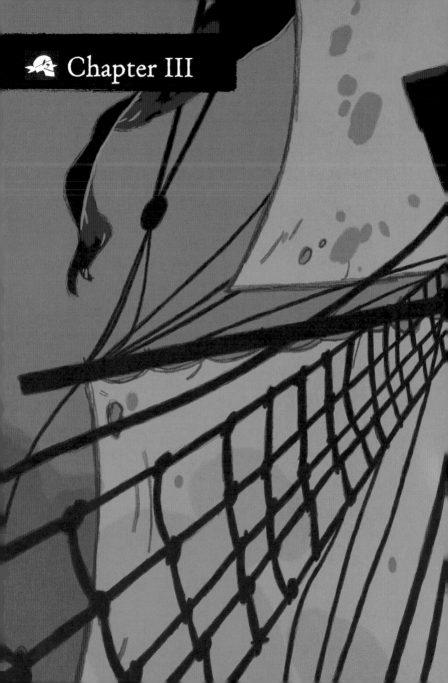

# Chapter III

# The *Flying Dutchman*

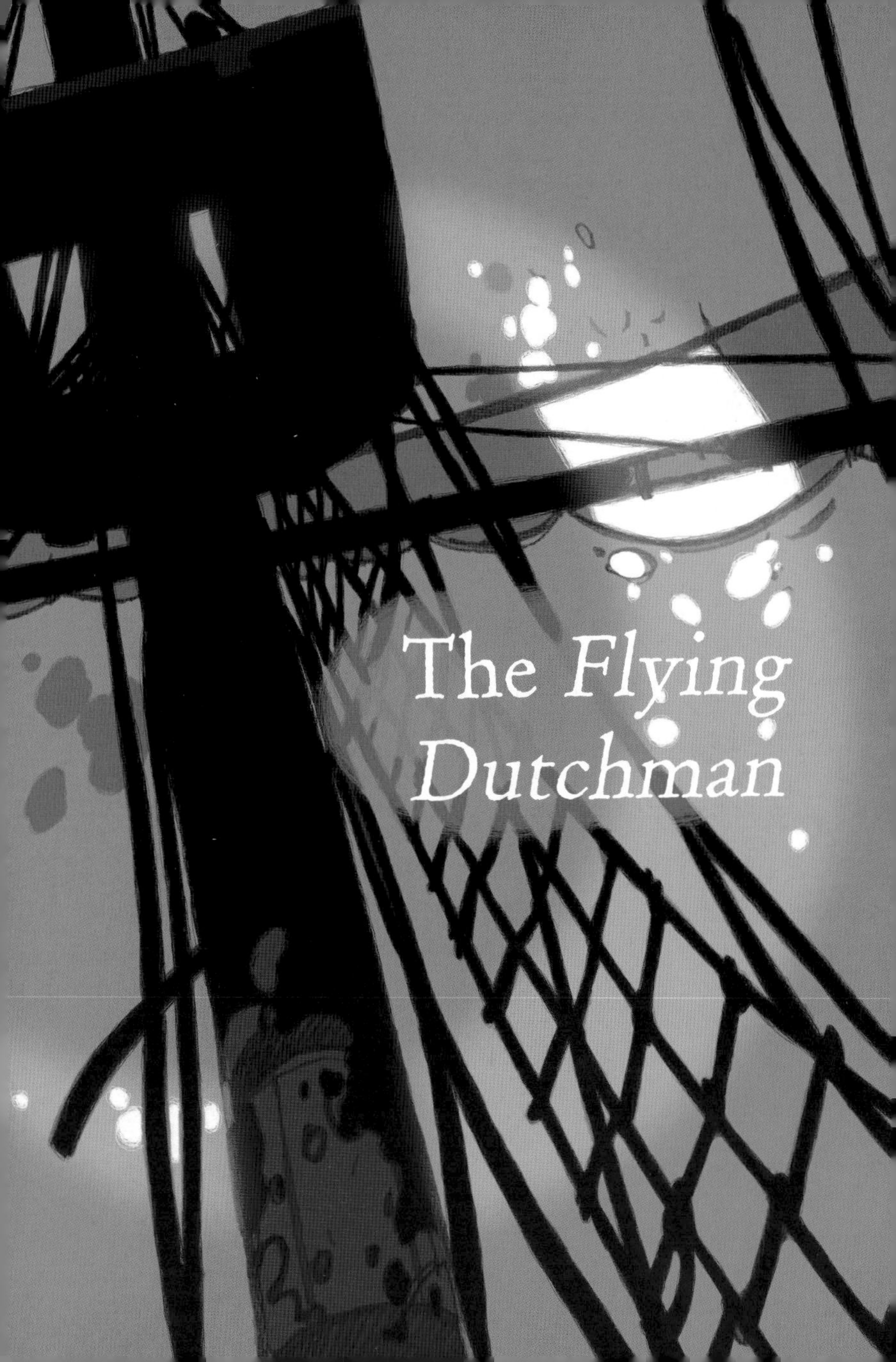

The ship slowly stopped pitching from side to side. The collision between the two vessels had been averted and the ship seemed to be back on course.

"If we'd fallen into the water, they'd never have found us!" Louise exclaimed.

"We'd have been crushed between the hulls. Flattened like pancakes..."

Just then the mast shook and the sails whipped open with a clatter that sounded like an evil laugh. Blood - red sails!

"But..." stammered an astonished Benjamin. "The *Angry Flea* doesn't have red sails!"

"And its sails were already up. We're on the other ship!"

They looked down at the fog-shrouded deck below and saw two motionless figures.

"What kind of ship is this, where nobody's working?" asked Benjamin.

"There must be sailors in the rigging," said Louise. "Sails don't go up by themselves."

Looking up, they saw shapes in the rigging. Suddenly one of them loomed larger. It was swinging on the end of a rope that had worked loose.

"Look out!" yelled Benjamin. "He's going to fall on top of us."

They just had time to dive out of the way as the sailor crash-landed between them, getting tangled up in the halyards.

"He must have knocked himself out," Louise thought, judging by the way the sailor hung there with his arms dangling.

She shook him by the shoulder and his hat fell off to reveal—a skull!

"Aargh!" she cried in terror.

"Aaaargh!" shrieked Benjamin, almost falling over backward.

"It's a skeleton! A skeleton dressed in sailor's clothing!"

They heaved him off the ropes. The skeleton flew backward, twirling round and round in a tangle of ropes. Shaking from head to toe, the children started to climb down from the halyards. Something tapped Benjamin's shoulder sharply. His scream stuck in his throat. He jumped and was about to flee, but his sister grabbed his arm and held him back.

"It's Shut-your-trap!"

Louise had to shout twice to her brother that it was only the parrot before he calmed down. Benjamin leaned his head against a piece of rigging—and let out a long, deep breath.

"The *Angry Flea* must be following us. Parabas hasn't abandoned us," he said, breathing another sigh of relief.

"Of course!" Louise agreed. "Otherwise, the parrot wouldn't be here."

Louise started to climb down, followed by Benjamin with the parrot on his shoulder.

"It was really scary finding that skeleton in the rigging!" Louise shivered. "I wonder why no one took it down?"

"Perhaps it was a punishment," Benjamin suggested. "That poor soul must have done something dreadful to be punished like that."

"Son of a sharrrk!" exclaimed Shut-your-trap! "They take discipline serrriously arrround herrre!"

Once on deck, they ran toward a sailor who was leaning over a hammock.

"Sir, we fell off the *An...*"

Louise quickly butted in to stop her brother giving away the name of the pirate ship.

"...off the, err... *Ant and Bee,*" she said, finishing his sentence. "When our ships collided we were thrown onto your ship."

The sailor didn't reply. He had his back toward them and was leaning forward as if looking out to sea.

"He must be deaf," muttered Benjamin.

He took hold of the man's sleeve and shook him.

"Hey, mister!"

The ship rolled slightly to one side. The man seemed to lurch backward, and as he swiveled around the children came face to face with the empty eye sockets of yet another skeleton. At once, Benjamin and Louise felt their hair stand on end and all the blood draining from their faces. They stared for a moment, gasping. There was another sudden roll of the ship and the skeleton flopped back into position across the hammock.

'Where on earth have we ended up?" stammered Louise.

They turned toward a gunner crouching near his cannon.

"He's a bag of bones, too!" Benjamin announced, after shaking him.

"And this one!" added Louise, spotting another raggedy skeleton sitting on a coil of rope, elbows on knees and pipe in hand.

"What's going on?" asked the boy, panic rising in his voice. "Do you think they were ill and died? Could we catch it too?"

Suddenly the wind blew up. The cloak of fog that had engulfed them broke up a little and the sea was now visible. The scene on board the *Flying Dutchman* was quite bizarre! Fully clothed skeletons were everywhere, as though frozen to the spot while going about their normal tasks. Three of them appeared to be hauling on a rope attached to a pulley, as if they were keeping the mainmast in place. Others sat on the yardarms, legs dangling in the air. Some were positioned alongside cannons as though ready to fire a broadside. Perched on the stairway leading to the poop deck was the skeleton of the cook, still holding a half-plucked chicken carcass.

"Look. Down there!" cried Louise suddenly. "I saw the wheel turn. The helmsman must be alive!"

They scrunched up their faces in disgust as they clambered over the bones of the cook to get to the poop deck, but they were disappointed when they reached the helm. A skeleton dressed in a tricorn hat and a rotting overcoat gripped the wheel with both hands. His lower jaw gaped open as if shouting out an order.

"He must be the captain," Benjamin guessed. "You can tell by the jewels on his neck and fingers. And he's got a boarding sword at his belt."

"Currrsed Dutchman!" squawked Shut-your-trap! "Ghost of a pirrrate! You'll take us all to hell with you!"

"Pirate?" gulped Benjamin.

Just at that moment, the flag at the top of the mast cracked like a thunderclap. The children stared up at it.

"Th… the Jolly Roger," mumbled Louise.

The skeleton's skull swayed in the wind; its deathly grimace looked like a blood-curdling smile.

"No sign of the *Angry Flea*," said Benjamin in a frightened voice.

"Parabas can't be far," his sister reassured him. "Let's try and attract his attention by firing a cannon. There must be some gunpowder among the stores, and there are cannonballs here on the deck."

"The cannon could blow up in our faces if we overload it," said Benjamin anxiously.

"Well, while you were learning about hoisting sails with On-the-Fence, I was working alongside the gunners on the *Angry Flea*. You may know all about map reading and directing maneuvers, but I know all about cannons. I know how to measure powder, how to pack the cannon with a ramrod, and how to fire the charge. It's easy."

"In theory, maybe… but is it easy to do?"

Louise grabbed her brother's hand and dragged him through the hatch and down between decks.

There were many more skeletons here, too—all fixed in various working positions. The children had to thread their way through them to reach the dimly lit storeroom.

Louise climbed out through the open hatchway with the powder measure and the ramrod. Benjamin followed with a barrel of gunpowder and some fuses. As she passed one of the skeletons, Louise grabbed a tinderbox from its hand.

"Yuk!" she shivered when she touched its bones. "Sorry, mate. I need this or I'll end up like you."

"End up like you!" repeated the parrot, flapping his wings. "In the devil's stew pot!"

"Hey, you—shut your trap!" the children growled in unison.

When they reached the deck, they wheeled one of the cannons back, but just as they were about to pour in some gunpowder, they noticed it was already loaded. Benjamin put the fuse in and lit it. The shot deafened them and there was the sound of splintering wood as the gun flew backward.

"We forgot to lift the gun cover!" groaned Louise, "and we never put the wooden chocks behind the wheels. That cannon could have crushed our feet!"

"Sorry, I was a bit hasty," admitted Benjamin. "I don't know much about guns."

Louise shrugged her shoulders.

"Never mind—let's get on with it! Let's check if they're all loaded, and this time we'll lift the covers and put chocks behind the wheels."

One after the other, each cannon discharged a cannonball, raising sprays of water on each side of the ship. It sounded like a thunderstorm, and the *Flying Dutchman* was now surrounded by thick gray smoke.

Shortly afterward, a rumbling sound came back in answer. It sounded as if a whole squadron had fired its weapons.

"See!" said a delighted Louise. "Someone's heard us."

"Look over there!" said Benjamin in a panicky voice. "That's a storm we're hearing, not a ship!"

Louise turned to look. Her eyes widened and her mouth fell open in horror. Over to the west, the heavens had turned black and were crisscrossed by blinding flashes of lightning.

"The devil's stew pot!" screeched Shut-your-trap! "We'rrre going to taste the soup of hell!"

# Chapter IV

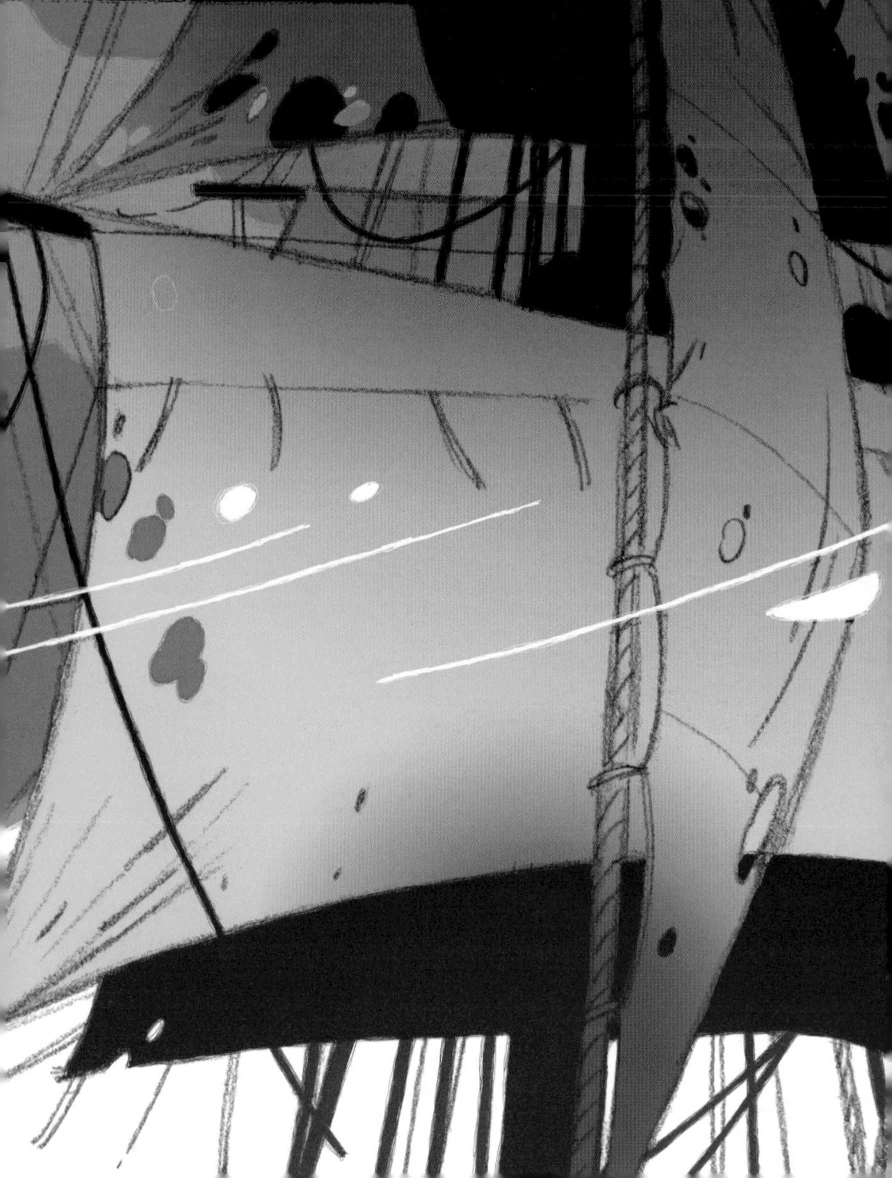

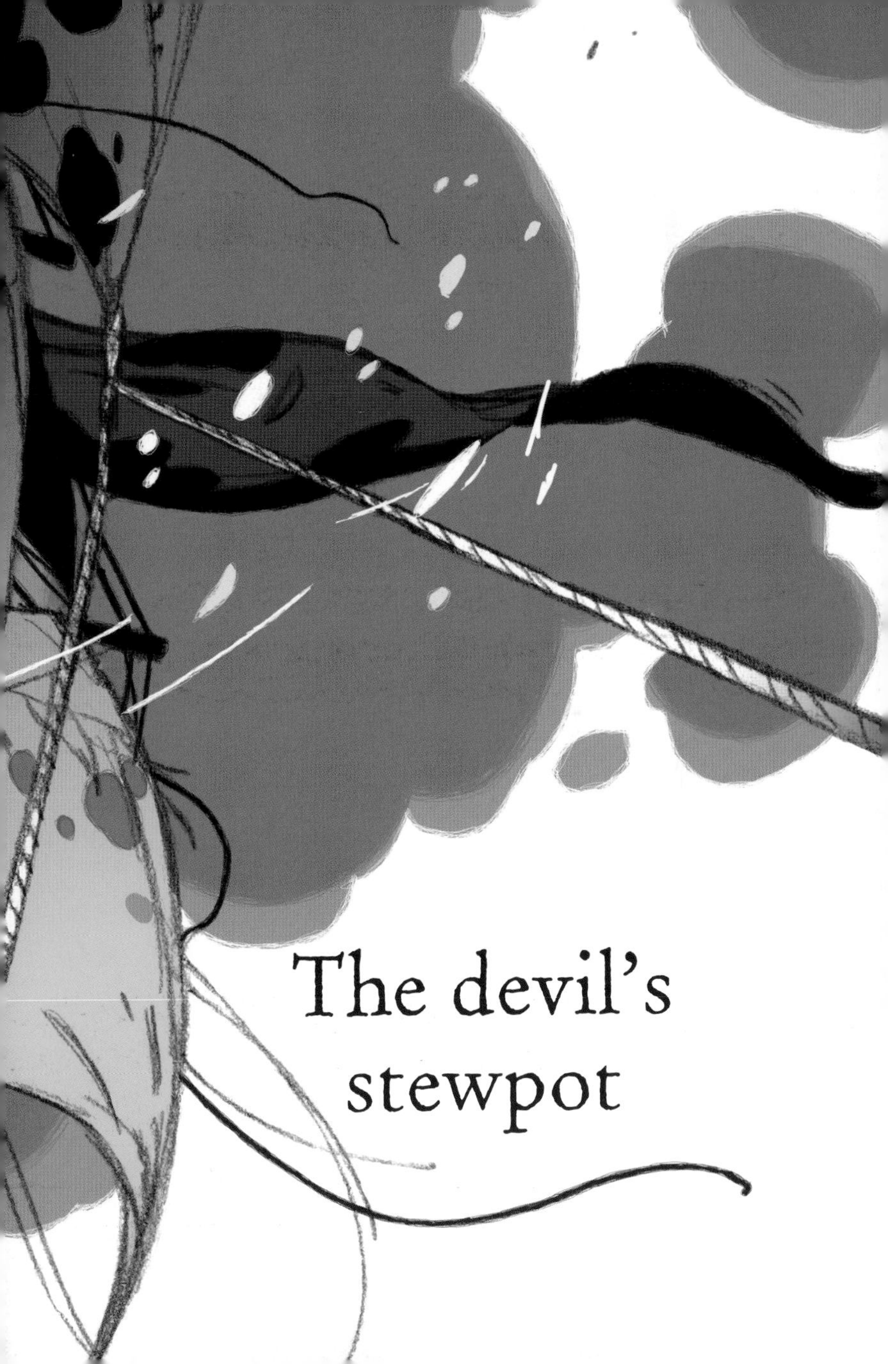

# The devil's stewpot

A whirlwind hit the ship and shook it as if trying to tear off its mast.

"It's a headwind," yelled Benjamin. "We need to tack."

"What does that mean?"

"We've got to meet the wind head-on. We need to put the sails up again or the ship could capsize!"

"What… on our own? Even if both of us pulled on the ropes, we're not strong enough to lift the canvas."

The sky had become even darker. The ship tossed about as the sea boiled and swelled with enormous white-crested waves. Every timber on the *Flying Dutchman* creaked.

"This time, I'm giving the orders!" Benjamin exclaimed. "I know what to do. I'll take the wheel and change course to put the wind behind us. The waves will toss the ship around like a nutshell, but it's the only way to stop her keeling over."

He raced to the wheel on the poop deck and tried to take hold of it without actually touching the captain's skeleton.

"Hurry up," called Louise, "the storm's almost on top of us!"

"Holy tobacco!" screamed the parrot in his shrill voice. "Son of a sharrrk! Shiverrr me timberrrs!"

Despite his revulsion, Benjamin grabbed hold of the wheel with both hands and tried to turn it. But it wouldn't budge. He leaned all his weight onto one of the crossbars on the wheel but still nothing happened. The wheel wouldn't move at all. The tattered skeleton looked as though it was sneering at him.

He yelled out, "I can't do it! It's stuck!"

Darkness crept over the sea. Flashes of lightning tore across the sky and skimmed the waves, followed by great crashes of thunder. The clouds parted. Rain as sharp as arrows began to lash down.

"It's impossible to steer," Benjamin told his sister, who had come to help him. "Somehow we've got to maneuver the ropes to get the sails side on to the wind."

But the halyards and the tiller were both as rigid as iron. Not one line or yard would turn in its pulley. In desperation, Benjamin swung on the ropes, trying against all odds to hoist the sails. He strained, cursed, swore, and hurled insults at the wretched boat.

"It's no good," said Louise. "This ship won't do what we want it to!"

Benjamin sensed the despair in his sister's voice. A huge wave swamped the *Flying Dutchman*. The prow of the ship rose, throwing her keel in the air. The twins and the skeleton crew were tossed head over heels, landing squashed against the stairway to the poop deck. Cannonballs rolled in all directions. Then the ship swung forward.

"Look out!" Benjamin bellowed to Louise. The girl leaped aside. A cannon had slipped from its chocks and was rolling toward them. It crushed one of the pirates, narrowly missed Louise, and plunged into a coil of ropes.

"Let's go up on the poop deck," Benjamin advised. "It's too dangerous down here."

Clutching onto ropes, they edged toward the rear platform, while Shut-your-trap! continued to shriek at the top of his voice that they were all going to drink the devil's soup. The cursed *Dutchman*'s captain, his overcoat flapping around him like a torn flag, was still tied to the wheel and somehow seemed to be enjoying the storm. The two children held tightly onto the bench behind him.

"The sword!" Louise shouted suddenly.

"What about it?"

Without answering, Louise grabbed the pirate's weapon, flung herself at the halyard which held the mainsail, and tried to cut through it.

"Give it to me!" her brother shouted. "I'm stronger than you."

He took the sword in both hands and started hacking at the rope.

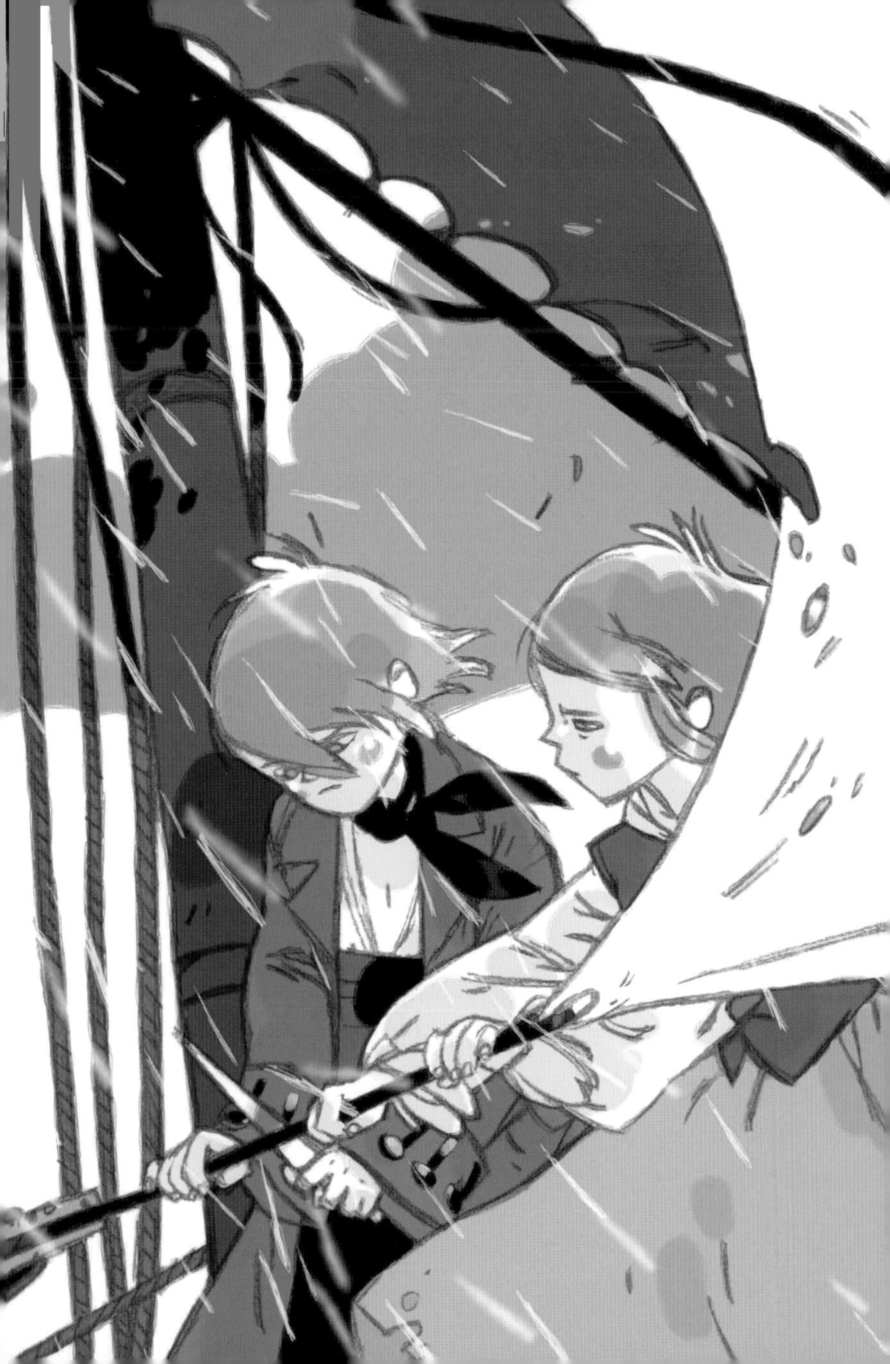

"Once we've cut through it, the sail won't hold up to the wind," he said.

But the rope wouldn't give. With every blow, the ship seemed to flinch as if in pain. It rolled, bucked, and pitched before falling back into the trough of a wave. Every timber shuddered.

"You'd think the ship itself was fighting back," said Louise.

Benjamin gave up. It was impossible to free the sails. Moments later he caught sight of a wall of water breaking over them with a terrible roar.

"We've had it!"

He and his sister wrapped their arms around the main mast and held onto each other tightly. The ship felt as though it were flying, then the sea swamped the decks. It pounded at the children as though trying to wrench them off. Choking and battered by the water, Benjamin and Louise only managed to hang on through sheer terror of letting go. The *Flying Dutchman* listed sharply, emptied the sea water from her decks, and then righted herself again. Louise had just caught sight of the pirate captain turning the wheel when a second wave crashed onto the deck. She lost hold of her brother's hand and was swept away by a wave as the ship dipped again.

"Nooo!" yelled Benjamin.

Seawater flowed in through the portholes. Sprays of water crashed down on the decking. Louise managed to grab hold of a cannon and its weight stopped her from being hurled overboard. The next wave dragged her back in the opposite direction. Her brother, who was still hanging on to a rope around the main mast, grabbed Louise by the leg, pulled her to him, and held her close to his chest.

"It was the *Dutchman*'s captain who turned the ship!" Louise gasped. "I saw him turn the wheel."

The sails were now parallel to the wind. The ship no longer faced the storm, but rocked from one rolling wave to another.

"So the captain still has a brain in his head! He's just saved his ship," said Benjamin.

At that moment, the tricorn hat began to move. Something was inside it!

"What on earth is it?" cried Louise.

"Let's shelter between decks," Benjamin suggested. "We can't do anything up here, and at least we can't be swept off by the waves down there." He turned cautiously toward the hatch, lifted the covers, and was about to go down when the captain's hat began to speak.

"By the devil! Get me out of herrre! I'm being eaten alive!"

"It's Shut-your-trap! He's been hiding under the captain's hat and he's got one of his claws stuck in the skeleton's jaw!"

Benjamin waited for the ship to come up out of a large wave, then climbed onto the poop deck to free the parrot and replace the skeleton's hat.

Between decks, the pirate skeletons had been thrown all over the place. The children sheltered under the stairway. Louise clutched her brother's hand, squeezing it hard.

"Do you think a ghost ship can sink?" she asked. Benjamin wasn't sure. He didn't even want to think about it. The *Flying Dutchman* had plunged into the trough of another wave and was just rearing up again. He felt as if his heart was in his mouth and an invisible hand was clutching his stomach tightly. Louise could hardly breathe. Every lurch, jolt, and convulsion of the ship filled her with rising anxiety.

"What will happen to us?" she asked in a scared voice. Benjamin shook his head. The ship reared up once again but this time it seemed to plunge forever.

"Aaaaah!" screamed the parrot. "We'rrre sinking. To the lifeboats! Hold on for dearrr life!"

It felt as if the end had come…

# Chapter V

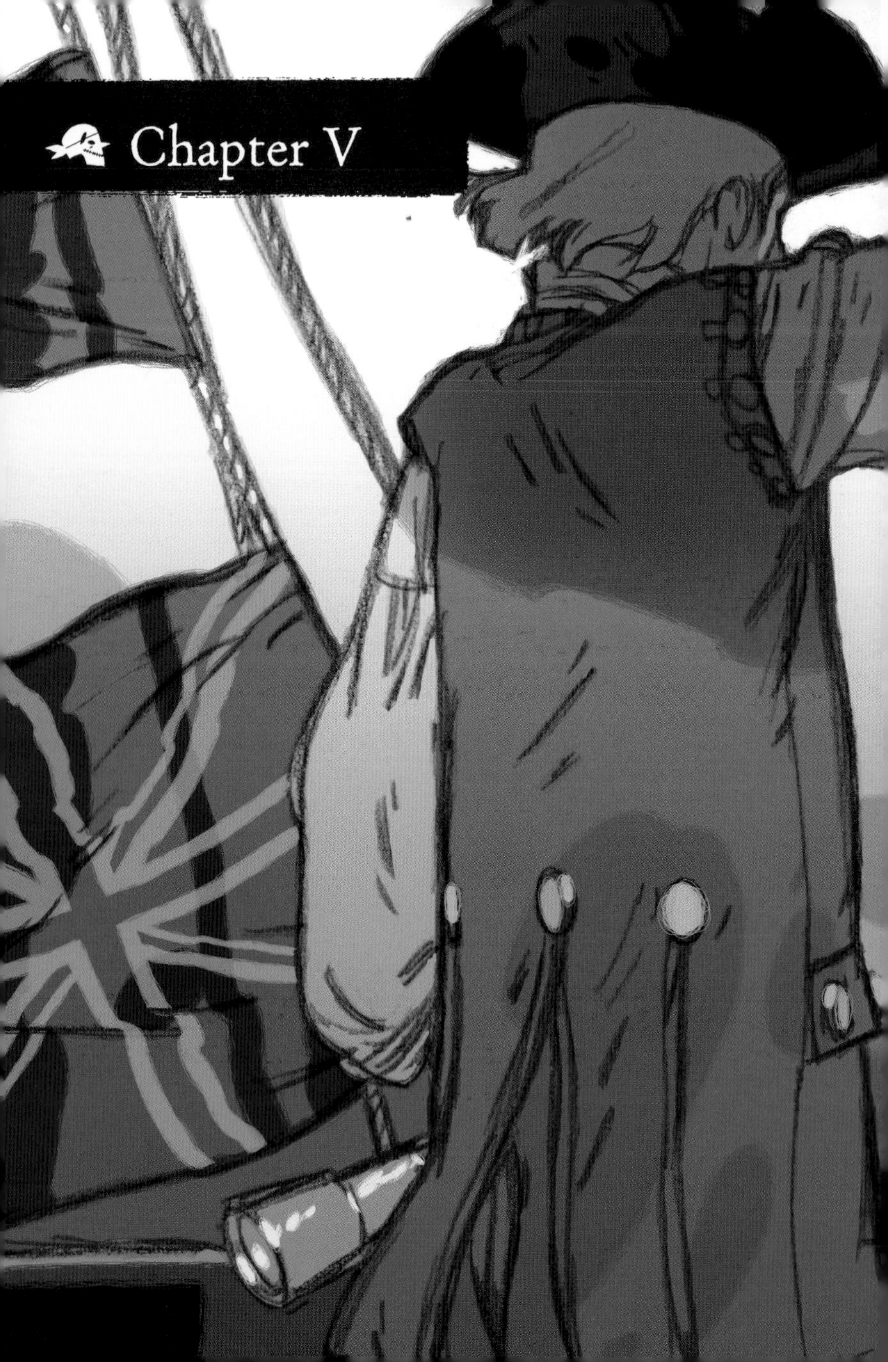

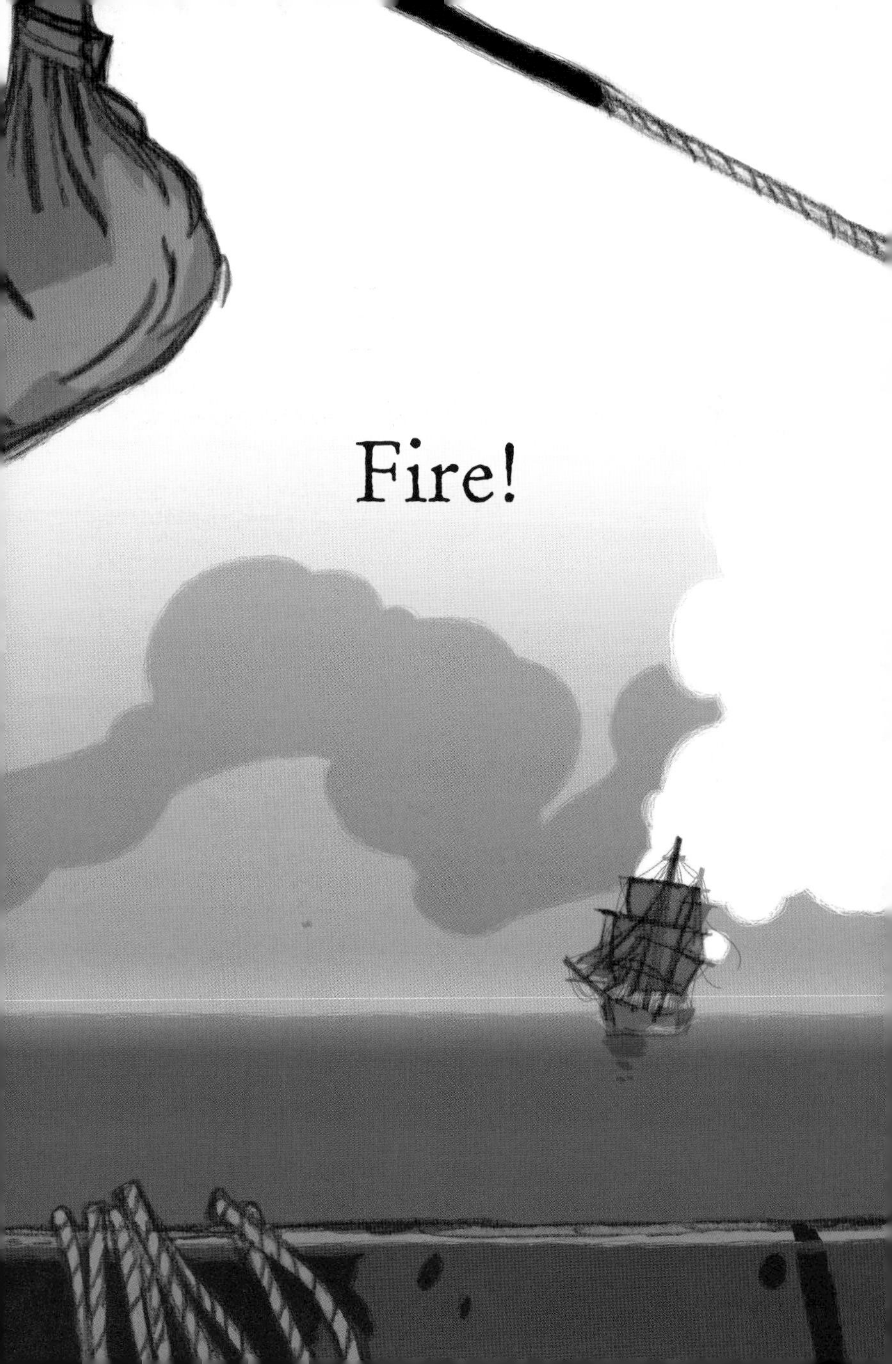
Fire!

But a ghost ship can't sink! In defiance of all storms, it rides the oceans wildly and skims over it like a seabird!

Eventually, the wind dropped and the waves died back. The water was still gray, but the sky slowly regained a little of its paradise blue. Benjamin and Louise went back on deck. Shut-your-trap! flew around the ship, as if to check for any damage to the *Flying Dutchman*.

"What now?" Louise sighed. "Perhaps we too are doomed to sail the oceans for all eternity."

"We're bound to come across other ships," Benjamin reassured her.

"But now that the *Flying Dutchman* has captured us, I'm sure he'll manage to evade them," Louise replied, nodding her head toward the cursed captain.

Benjamin looked around. The sea was completely empty, so desperately empty that he wondered if the storm had destroyed every other ship. Where was the *Angry Flea*?

"We'll have to attract other ships!" muttered Louise.

The parrot settled on Benjamin's shoulder, shrieking "I'm hungrrry! I want my rrration. My rrration, son of a sharrrk!"

"Go and pick on the pirates' bones then" Benjamin muttered, brushing him away.

"Rrr... I'm starrrving. Scoundrrrel! Rrrascal!"

"I've got it!" cried Louise, rubbing her hands.

"What... rations? I doubt if there's anything edible left in the storeroom. We'll just have to eat this noisy bird."

On hearing this, Shut-your-trap! flew off with a great flapping of wings to perch in the rigging.

"Murrrderrrerrr! Cutthrrroat! Cannibal! Rrr!"

"I've thought of a way to send out a signal,"

Louise explained. "We'll set fire to the sails! The smoke will be visible for miles…"

"…and we'll sink lock, stock, and barrel if no one sails into these waters," her brother finished.

"So, would you rather stay here and wait till your body shrivels and your skin peels off? You said it yourself—there are only bones to pick at here. Well?"

Benjamin hesitated. His sister was right. They had to get off this cursed ship as soon as possible.

"I saw tar-soaked oakum in the weapon store," recalled Louise. "We can put it near all the sails. It'll burn like mad."

It didn't take them long to carry out this plan, then Louise brought out the tinderbox. Whoosh! The oakum caught fire and long flames soon leapt up toward the sails. A thick white plume of smoke coiled upward from the wet canvas.

"Arrrsonists! Rrroasterrrs!" exclaimed the parrot, hopping from foot to foot.

Flying sparks ignited the ropes. Soon, all the masts were burning too. The ship crackled and groaned but continued to plow its course on the sea, now tinged orange by the flames.

"Ship ahoy!" Shut-your-trap! squawked suddenly from the bowsprit.

The children hurried on deck, their hearts pounding. A tiny speck was visible on the horizon.

"No, it's three ships!" Benjamin called out beneath the flames.

Shielding their eyes with their hands, they watched the ships get closer.

"They're making good speed," said Louise. "It won't be long before they reach us."

The ships got bigger as they cut a path toward the *Flying Dutchman*.

"They're frigates," Benjamin exclaimed, seeing their three masts, "but I can't make out their flags."

"Flags!" shouted Louise. "They'll see the Jolly Roger flying on our ship and fire at us!"

They looked up, hoping that the flag had burned. But no! The skull and crossbones pirate flag flew boldly above the flames.

The twins ran toward the halyard that raised and lowered the flag, but it wouldn't budge in its pulley.

"We could wave and call for help," suggested Benjamin. "If they see us through their telescopes, perhaps they won't fire!"

They raced up onto the poop deck and jumped up and down, waving their arms. The three frigates drew closer.

"They're English!" Benjamin suddenly declared, recognizing their colors.

The ships fanned out and presented their guns.

"They're going to fire!" gasped Louise. "They must think the pirates have set a trap for them and are preparing to board."

The *Flying Dutchman* suddenly dipped—her figurehead and bowsprit disappeared under the water.

"Aaargh!" screamed the children as they fell overboard.

As the bow of the ship disappeared beneath the waves, the stern reared up, and the ship rolled for a moment before plunging into the depths. Stirred up by the wash, the sea boiled and bubbled. Shut-your-trap! screeched out, "Two pirrrates overrr-boarrd!"

Their heads bobbed up. A launch had come over from one of the frigates. It soon reached the children and strong arms lifted them on board. The sailors and the children had barely returned to the frigate when the Jolly Roger emerged above the water. Masts, sails, and ropes then began to rise from the ocean. Water cascaded from the *Flying Dutchman* as it surfaced with its flames extinguished. The sailors were dumbstruck. By the time the squadron commander had reacted, it was too late to give the order to fire. The ghost

ship had tacked between two of the frigates and, sailing before the wind, it had gained speed and was pulling away from them in full sail.

"It's the *Flying Dutchman*!" exclaimed the commander in English. "What were you doing on that ship?"

Benjamin and Louise didn't answer. They looked like two bedraggled fish washed up on deck, and they didn't understand English at all.

"We're French," said Louise. "From Paris."

"So you're enemies of England," declared the officer in French. "Who is your father?"

"Cap'n Rrroc!" crowed the parrot. "The grrreatest pirrrate in the Carrribean!"

"You don't say!"

"No!" cried Benjamin. "Our father is dead and we were deckhands on the *Angry Flea* before…"

He stopped and bit his tongue, aware of his blunder. Too late! Louise closed her eyes and shrugged her shoulders.

"That's Black Beard's ship. This gets better and better! So you were being trained as pirates, eh?" snapped the officer, looking them over from head to toe. "I should hang you from the yardarm of my ship, but as you're just children I'll content myself with locking you up in jail when we reach Jamaica. My squadron is bound for Port Royal to reinforce the garrison on the island. Hey, leading seaman!"

he yelled out in English. "Put these two in the hold and keep them there till we reach the island. As for how they were on the ghost ship—well, no doubt that's some buccaneer mischief. I'll interrogate them later."

"Billy goat's horrrn! Parrrabas won't be happy…" shrieked Shut-your-trap! as the sailor shoved the children toward the hold. "He'll come afterrr them! He'll be verrry angrrry!"

"Tell the cook to catch that frightful bird and pluck it!" the officer ordered his second mate.

"Murrrderrrerrr! Skinnerrr!" the parrot screeched in English, as it flew up to the ship's highest sail.

"Well, at least we know he speaks more than one language," said the officer, turning on his heel and returning to his cabin.

# Chapter VI

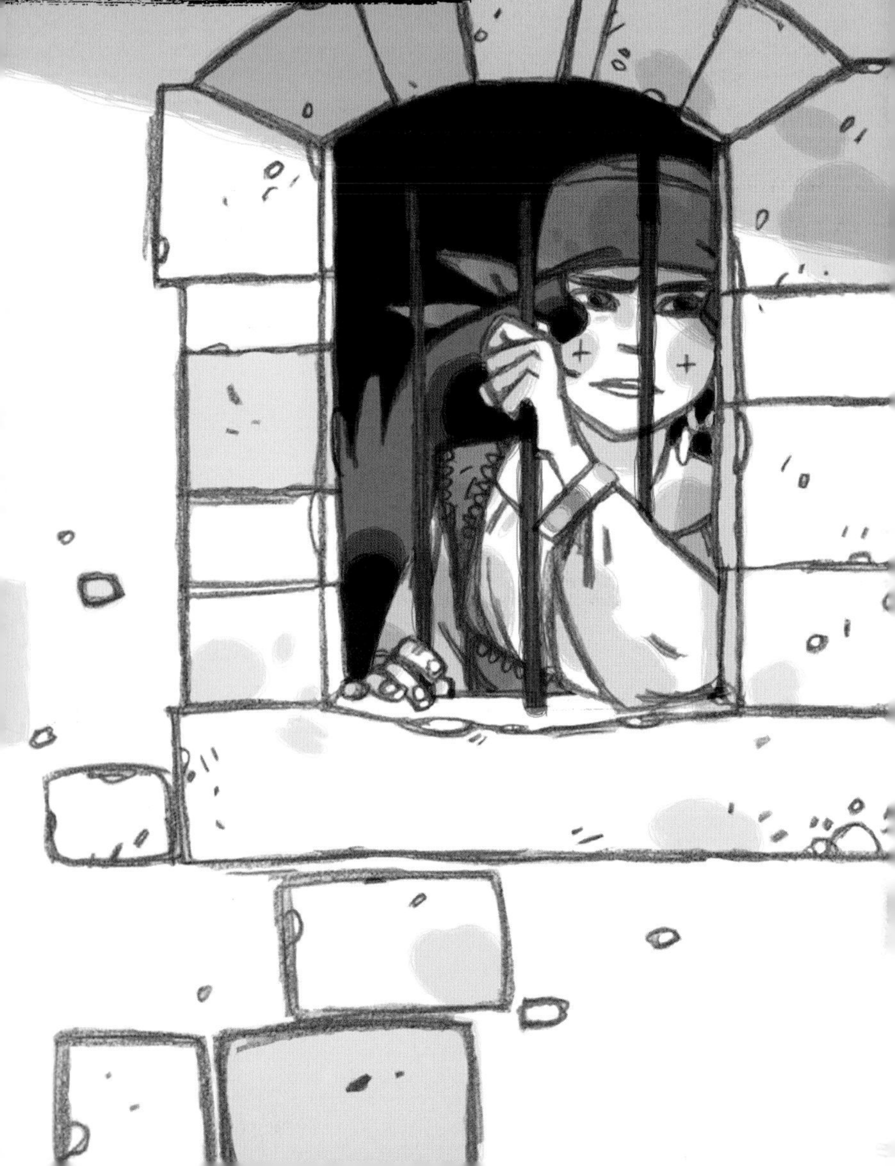

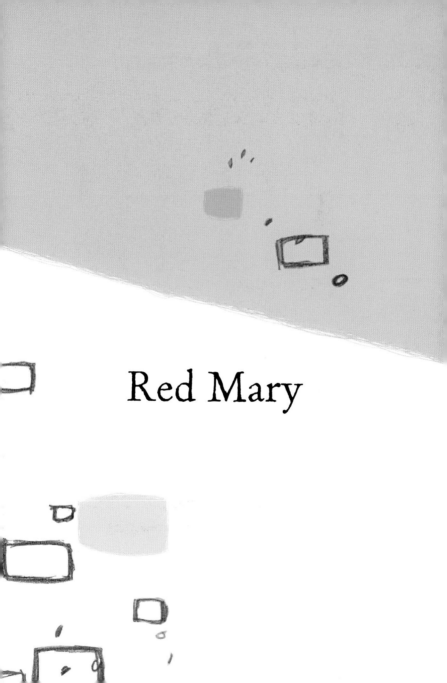

Red Mary

Situated at the end of a spit of land on the south coast of Jamaica, Port Royal protected Kingston harbor—a calm stretch of water that separated the town from the sea. Scattered along the coast were wooden shacks shaded by palm trees, but the main town was clustered around a church built by the Spanish and an imposing fort that protected the harbor entrance. Cannons protruded over the walls of the battlements. Benjamin and Louise had been moping around in the fort since the previous evening.

Louise held on to the bars of their cell window as she watched ships entering and leaving the harbor.

"I wonder where Shut-your-trap! has wound

up?" Benjamin wondered aloud. "We haven't seen him since we were locked in the hold."

"He'll have flown off in search of other parrots on the island."

"I hope nothing's happened to him. I was just getting used to having him around!"

"Me, too," confessed Louise. "And he would have helped us get back to the *Angry Flea*. Now we really are on our own."

"Yes," agreed her brother. "We're worse off now than we were in Paris. We know who our father is now, but we're certainly paying a price for it!"

A door creaked on its hinges and footsteps echoed along the tunnel leading to the dungeons. A man stopped in front of their cell door and looked at the children through the grille. Then he took a bunch of keys from his belt, inserted one of them into the lock, and opened the cell door.

"Out!" he snapped in French.

"You're… are you letting us go?" asked Benjamin.

"The governor doesn't want kids aged less than fifteen years old in these jails," the jailer grunted. "But don't think for one moment that he's releasing you to become pirates. No, you'll be kept in the fort to help old Shelsey. You, my lad, will become a soldier, and as for you, lass, you'll be a cook or a washerwoman. That'll keep you both on the straight and narrow. Cap'n Roc's brats, eh?"

"Cook or washerwoman?" Louise retorted. "Why can't we both be soldiers?"

"It's only female pirates that take up arms—like Red Mary who's banged up in a cell over there. Look where that got her!" the man scoffed as he grabbed Louise by the shoulder to make her move faster.

"You speak French really well," Benjamin remarked. "I thought only officers..."

"It pays a man to know several languages, here" the jailer interrupted. "The Spanish used to be in charge here and now it's the English. And the French islands are very close. You two will learn quickly. Old Shelsey even knows some of the local Caribbean dialect."

Old Shelsey turned out to be a hunchbacked old

man with a head like an upturned pear. He had a penetrating gaze that seemed to search the depths of your soul.

"These two won't molder long within these walls," he thought, when the jailer brought the children to him. "They're seabirds!"

"If these two escape, we'll recapture 'em and it'll be the rope for you, m' boy, and a life sentence for your sister!" warned the jailer menacingly, as though reading Shelsey's mind.

"I do a bit of everything around the fort," Shelsey told them when the jailer had gone back to his post, "from fetching wood to mending locks. You two can show me how you handle a weapon, for a start."

"A weapon?" queried Louise with a big grin. "A rapier? A saber? Or a pistol?"

"A broom!" barked the old man, handing one to each of them.

Benjamin and Louise spent the next few hours working themselves into the ground, cleaning the courtyard. Red-uniformed soldiers, marching from one building to another, forced them to leap out of the way. These were the recruits, the commander's newly arrived squadron. A sergeant major was yelling at them, trying to get them to march in step. Louise finally threw down her broom.

"There's no point in carrying on!" she exclaimed. "These redcoats keep marching through the dirt we've already swept up—they're spreading it all over the courtyard again. We didn't suffer storms and ghost ships to end up here as servants for the English!"

"But what can we do?"

"This is what I'm going to do!" she said, and grabbing the broom from her brother she set it on her shoulder like a rifle.

"One two! One two! One two!" she chanted as she kicked over a pile of rotting fruit that they had just swept up. "Hmm, you'd think we were English, too," she added cheekily.

Suddenly, old Shelsey's voice rang out.

"Hey, you two! I'll show you how to hold a broom by the right end!"

Taken by surprise, Louise slipped.

"Say what you like," she muttered between gritted teeth, "the first chance I get, this broom will end up in the baker's oven."

"And then Shelsey will make us clean the courtyard with our bare hands," whispered Benjamin. "Remember what happened to us on the Angry Flea? We had to use our shirttails!"

"You can carry on with sweeping later," ordered the old man. "For now your job is to take the prisoners their food. Follow me to the kitchens."

"What about us? When are we going to eat?"

"When the courtyard is clean!" retorted Shelsey.

Shortly afterward, the children were teetering along a corridor leading to the cells, carrying two huge vessels, one with fresh water and the other full of lentil broth. The jailer took them down to where the male prisoners were kept, then he told them to find their own way down the tunnel leading to the women's cells, where they themselves had been locked up. Red Mary was the only prisoner there. Aged about 25, the young woman had skin that was noticeably bronzed like the pirates on the *Angry Flea*.

Her long black hair hung down from the red scarf she always wore, which had given her the nickname of "Red Mary." Benjamin and Louise filled her mug and bowl through the iron bars of her cell door. As they were about to go, she asked:

"They call you Cap'n Roc's children. Why's that?"

"Because he's our father!" said Benjamin in a sarcastic tone.

"Really? Can you prove it?"

He was about to reply, but Louise stepped in front of him.

"What's it got to do with you?" she asked. "Do you know him?"

"Maybe I do."

"Did he tell you about us?"

Mary made a vague gesture.

"He did say he'd left a wife and twins in France, but I didn't believe him. As far as I'm concerned, inventing a family was his way of forming a bond with his home country. In reality, the ocean's his only country and his crew are his only family! Passing yourselves off as Cap'n Roc's children— well, I suppose it gives you a certain status..."

"You're wrong!" shouted Benjamin. "We are his children! We've got proof..."

His hand shot to his neck to bare the tattoo

on his shoulder. But Louise's warning kick made him hesitate for a moment and he scratched his shoulder instead. But Red Mary hadn't missed his reaction. She frowned and pursed her lips. Her eyes narrowed and her gaze became steely. Even her voice changed as she asked:

"Proof? Do you have proof?"

"You wouldn't believe us, so what's the point?" retorted Louise. She grabbed the vessel she'd been carrying and gestured to Benjamin that they had to go.

"Wait!"

The children shrugged their shoulders and started to move off.

"Wait! I know Cap'n Roc well. If you really are his children, I'll take you to him."

Mary had suddenly softened. Pressing her forehead against the bars she seemed to be begging the youngsters to listen to her.

"You'll take us to him?" sneered Benjamin, turning round. "Do you have a secret passage in your cell or something?"

"Get me out of this prison and I promise, on my word as a pirate, to lead you to his hideout."

Slowly, Louise walked back to her, the empty vessel in her arm.

"Once you're out, what then? You'll vanish! What's brought about this sudden change of tune? We know very well that our father is hiding on the island of Tortuga. We'll find him without your help."

Footsteps could be heard in the tunnel. The jailer appeared, his bunch of keys at his belt.

"What's going on?" he snarled. "How long does it take to pour a ladle of broth into a bowl?"

"Little cow!" spat Mary, her lip curling as she stared straight at Louise. "You're hardly past the age of being fed with cow's milk!"

"Ha, ha," laughed the jailer. "I love the way you pirates talk to each other. Get back outside, you two. Old Shelsey's waiting for you. I think he's got a little job for you to finish before you eat."

He smiled at them mockingly and mimed a sweeping action.

Once outside the building, Benjamin was burning to ask, "Why did you say that father's hideout was on Tortuga? You know very well he's not there!"

"I wanted to be sure that Red Mary wasn't trying to trick us."

"What do you mean?"

"She really does know where father is."

"She didn't say any such thing."

"Oh, yes she did! She knew I was testing her. She put me right by saying the word "cow" twice."

"Of course!" said Benjamin, slapping his forehead. Now he understood. "Île à Vache, or 'Cow Island' in English, is opposite Les Cayes, the town where father goes when he returns from his expeditions. Red Mary couldn't speak openly in front of the jailer... but surely we're not going risk setting her free?" he asked in a doubtful voice.

"Oh dear!" sighed Louise. "It's Shelsey. I'd like to stuff this broom down his throat!"

# Chapter VII

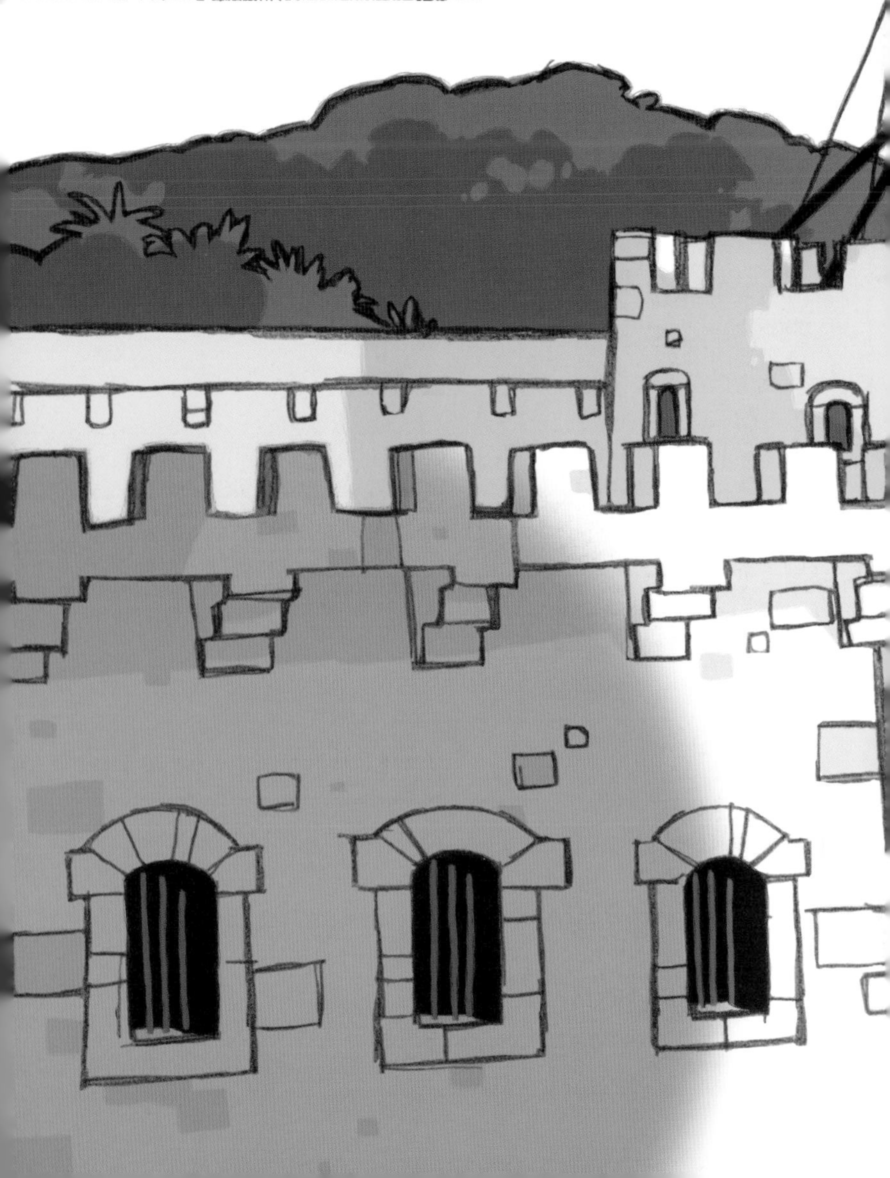

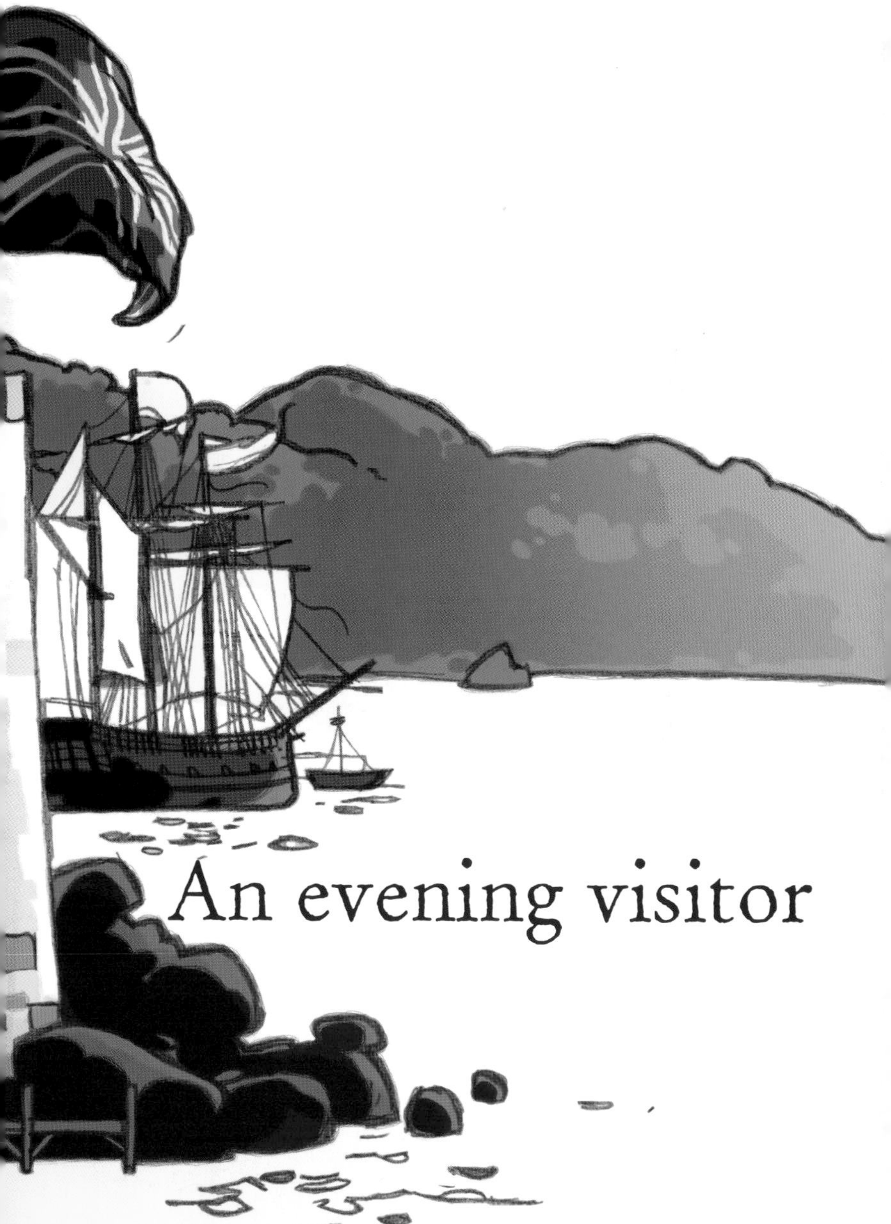

# An evening visitor

The days passed by living alongside Shelsey in a cubbyhole next to his room. Days spent wielding brooms around the courtyard, scouring the water ducts, taking meager rations to the prisoners, and putting up with Red Mary's smoldering anger as she kept trying to persuade them to free her.

"You're not planning to spend the rest of your lives here, are you?" she kept asking, trying to provoke them to escape. "But if you try to get out of here on your own, it will come to nothing. You don't know any hiding places in this town or around it. You'll never get to Hispaniola or Les Cayes. You won't even get out of Port Royal. And you know what fate awaits you if you're recaptured!"

Louise and Benjamin decided to ignore her. Red Mary struck the bars on her cell door in anger, shook them as if trying to tear them out, and threw her bowl at the wall.

"My fingers stink of rotten fish," Louise complained one evening. The twins were watching the sun setting over the sea before settling down to their meager supper. "My whole body stinks from wading around in rubbish."

"Me, too," groaned Benjamin. "I wish I could shed my skin like a snake!"

"I'd like to be a snake—to slide between the stones to get out of here."

"Shelsey would see us."

"Shelsey, the jailer, the soldiers... I'd like to know how Red Mary thinks she can get us all out of this fort. She must have a plan, or she wouldn't have offered to take us with her."

"You're not about to be taken in by that woman, are you?" asked Benjamin, worriedly. "She knows who we are only because I was stupid enough to mention the word 'proof' and reach for my shoulder. She must have known that Cap'n Roc's twins had bits of the treasure map tattooed on their shoulders. We've talked about it since. It's the pieces of the map she wants. It's father's treasure she's after. She'll kill us and then cut the tattooed skin from our shoulders."

"I don't trust Red Mary either," admitted Louise, "but our fate is linked with hers. We'll remain stuck in this fort as long as she's imprisoned here. And then, of course, she claims to know father."

Benjamin fell silent. He had no arguments to put to his sister.

"So it's decided," he muttered, "we're going to risk our lives?"

Louise didn't reply. Her eyes were fixed on the gold-tinged horizon.

"When I think of what we're about to do..." Benjamin began again. He didn't go on. His sister put her arm around his shoulders protectively.

"Father's there," she reassured him. "In the setting sun!"

"If he is in Les Cayes or on Île à Vache,

you're looking in the wrong direction!" Benjamin corrected her. "It's over there," he said, pointing behind him in an easterly direction, to where the night sky was drawing in. "I really did study those charts while you were fighting with Parabas on the *Angry Flea*," he said.

Louise responded with a mock sword fight. To her, the idea of escape symbolized adventure.

"So when do we go?" asked Benjamin.

Louise shrugged her shoulders slightly, as if to say she didn't know. Something gray suddenly landed right in front of them on the windowsill. They were so startled that they jumped and let out a cry.

"Action stations! All hands on deck! Parrrabas is back!"

Shut-your-trap! stopped to rub his beak with his claws, then lifted his head, puffed out his breast, and started shrieking again:

"Parrrabas is…"

"Shh!" Louise warned, catching him by the neck. "You'll alert the guards."

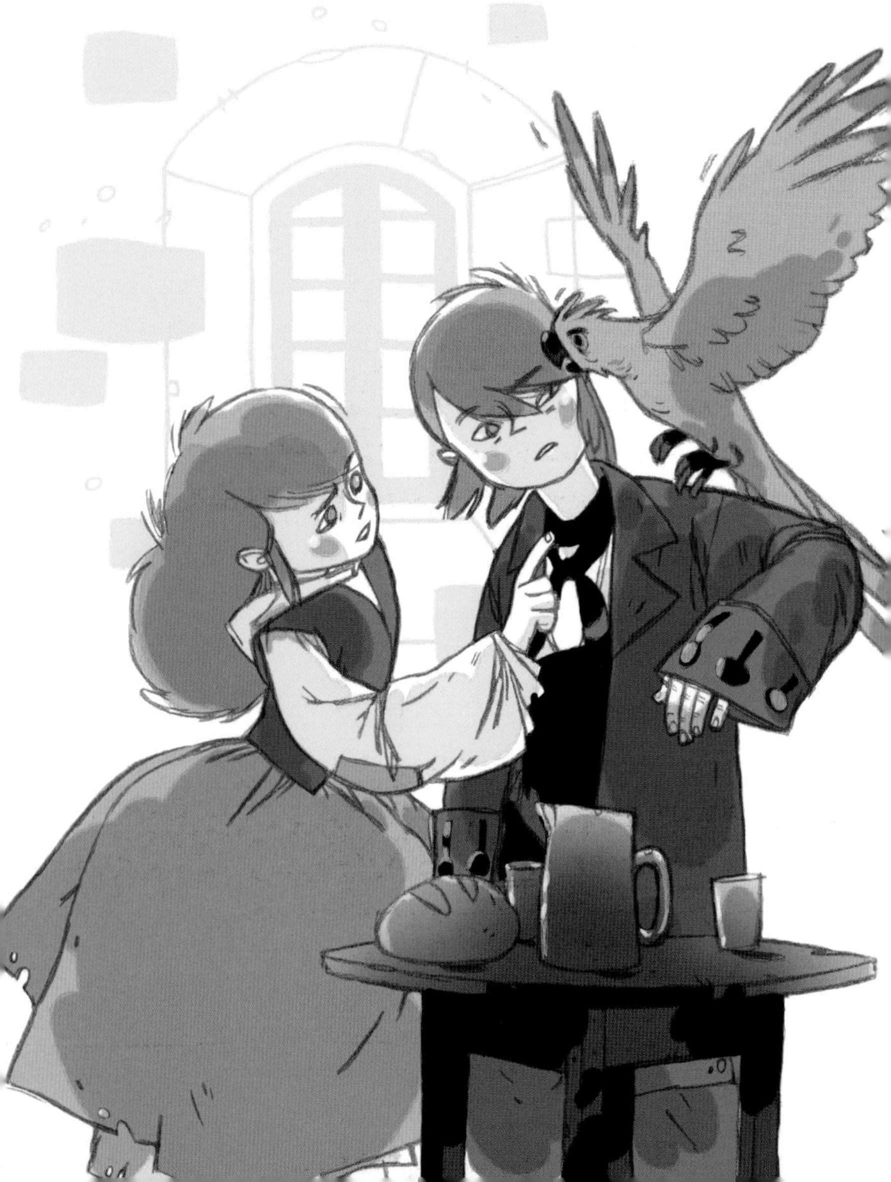

"Rrrououou!"

"Where is Parabas?" whispered Benjamin.

"Rrrououou!"

"Is he waiting for us somewhere?"

"Rrrououou!"

"Is he here now? Is he coming tomorrow? Or Later?"

"Rrrououou!"

"You're a pretty useless messenger!" complained Louise. "Repeat what the Marquis said to you."

"Rrrououou!"

"You've upset him," said Benjamin. "We won't get anything out of him now. You have to be gentle with him."

But Louise did just the opposite. Scowling and shaking the bird, she hissed: "Open your trap, you sack of feathers! Or I'll hang you from the yardarm!"

"Strrranglerrr! Trrraitorrr! Midnight! Two cable's lengths east..." spluttered the parrot.

"So the *Angry Flea* will anchor tonight, east of this land spit," Benjamin confirmed.

"Go back to Parabas," Louise ordered the parrot. "Tell him to approach the fort in a rowboat. The forrrt! In a rrrowboat! Understand? Repeat it after me. The forrrt! In a rrrowboat!"

"Rrrouououou!"

"For heaven's sake!" groaned Louise.

Benjamin put his hand on his sister's arm. "He's not stupid. He's a marvelous messenger."

"Marrrvelous! Admirrrable! Extrrraorrrdinarrry!" added Shut-your-trap! before flying off to sea, calling over and over again "The forrrt! In a rrrowboat! Son of a sharrrk!"

"Well?" the boy asked.

"That's it then. We'll escape tonight with Red Mary. If Parabas is waiting for us at sea, she's the only one that can get us out of the fort. Trust me. I'm good at this kind of adventure!"

# Chapter VIII

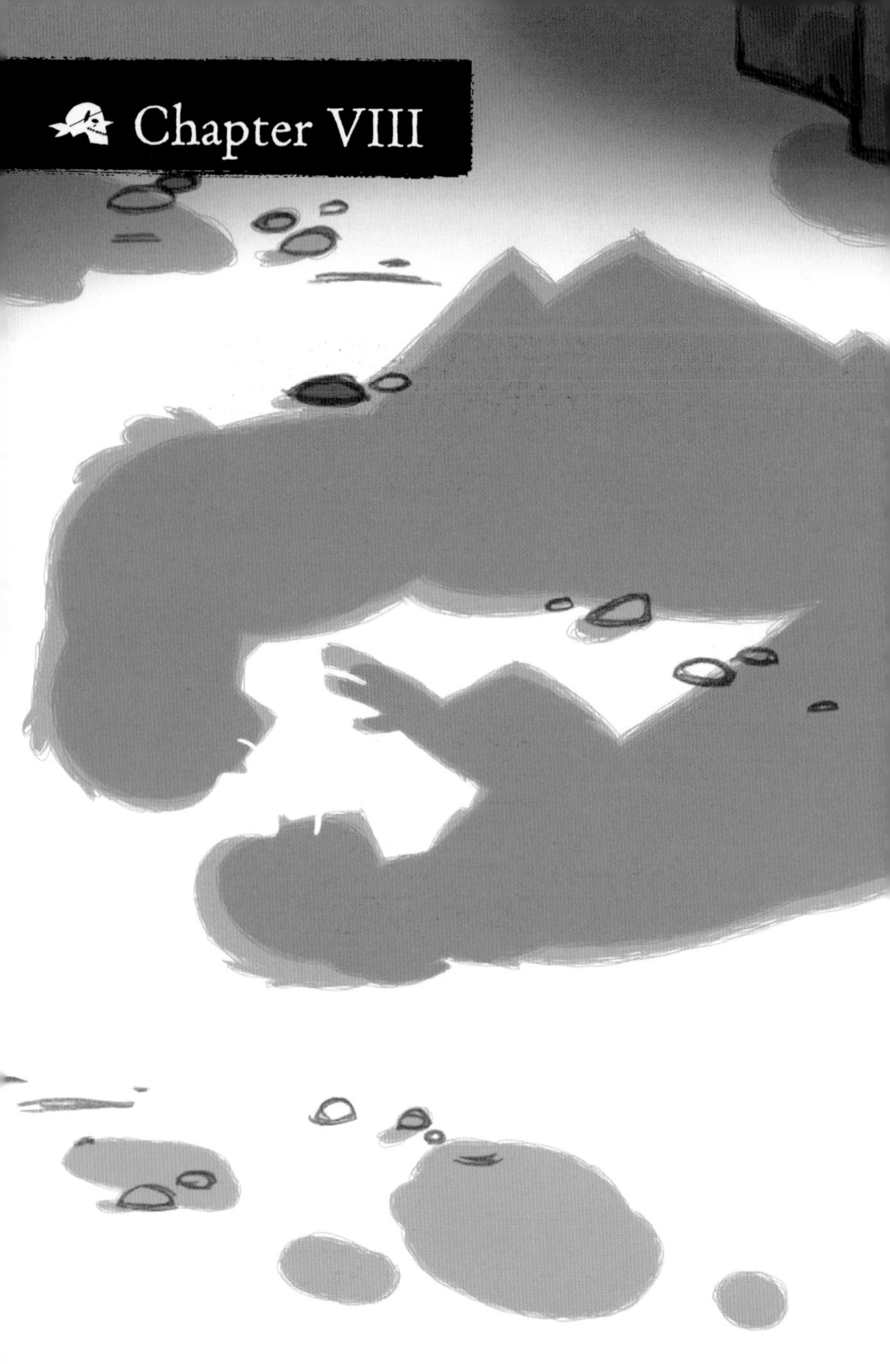

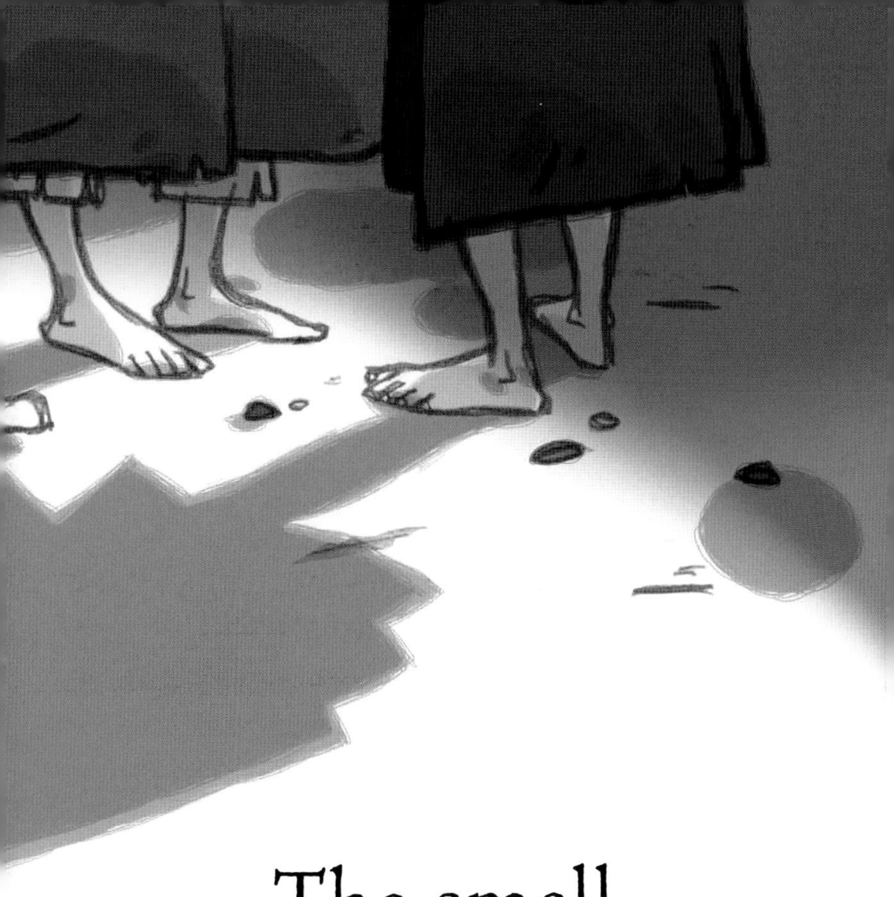

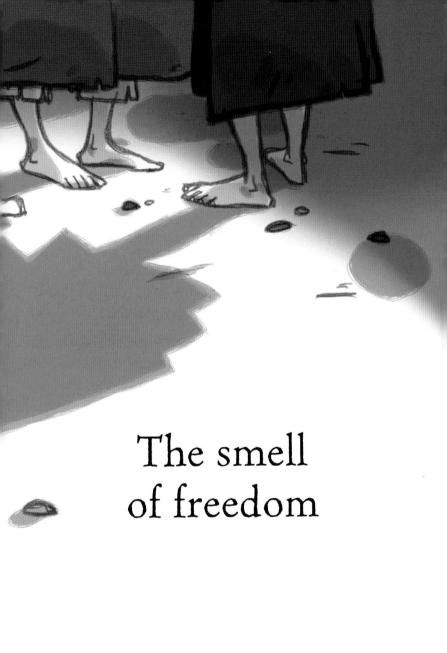

# The smell of freedom

Two shadows appeared on the wall near the prison.

"Are you sure Shelsey was really asleep?"

"He's snoring like a 100-cannon salute. I watched him finish a flagon of rum last night."

With a quick glance around to check that the sentries weren't watching the courtyard, the children sneaked into the building where the prisoners were kept. Clutching small lamps, they crept down a long corridor that twisted and turned until it reached a flight of steps up to the jailer's post. Halfway up the steps, they tied a wire across the staircase. Then Benjamin hid around the corner to wait in ambush, a large stone in his hand. Louise went up to the big studded door and knocked hard on it to raise the jailer from his makeshift bed, where he slept fully clothed. She heard grumbling and then movement. The door half-opened and a less than welcoming face peered out.

"What do you want?" he growled.

"Shelsey sent me to fetch you. He's got something important to tell you."

"At this hour? Is he mad?"

"It's a secret—something he wants to cover up. Something about a mistake you've made. The fort commander is furious and Shelsey thinks you'll be in hot water tomorrow!"

"A mistake?" The man looked stunned. "I haven't…"

Louise cut him off. "Shelsey said you've got to hurry. It's serious."

"I don't understand," said the man, scratching his head.

"Shelsey'll explain it all. He said he can help you out, but he needs to talk it over with you first. That's all I know."

The jailer bustled along the corridor, grumbling as he racked his brains to understand.

As he bolted down the stairs he suddenly flew head over heels, cursing loudly as he went, before landing on his stomach at the bottom. Straightaway Benjamin leaped out of the shadows and dealt him a heavy blow on the head that knocked him out cold. Louise and Benjamin turned him over, undid

his belt, and took his bunch of keys.

"Stay here. I won't be long. If he comes round…" Louise made a punching gesture.

Holding a lamp in her outstretched hand, she made her way toward the women's section of the prison and followed the long tunnel that eventually led to Red Mary's cell. The young woman was on her feet in an instant. She wasted no words, just "Ah, it's you! So you finally made up your mind!"

There was a clicking sound as the key turned in the lock. The cell door swung open. Following one another, they ran down the tunnel and joined Benjamin at the bottom of the stairs.

"From now on, I'll lead the way," declared Mary. "No arguments. And no lamp!" she ordered, smashing it on the head of the jailer, who had begun to stir.

The three of them then left the building. They slipped through the shadows, through the soldiers' dormitory… and on toward the latrines. "Shh!" breathed Mary, putting her finger to her lips to stifle their protests.

"This is disgusting!" Louise whispered. "I'm not going in there!"

"The latrines run off directly into the sea," Mary explained. "I had the chance to check this place out before I was captured."

"But we're not going to squeeze out through a, err... a hole, are we?"

"Don't worry. There's a skylight in the wall and there are no bars on it. I'll hoist you up onto the windowsill. Once in the water, we'll swim toward the harbor. My ship, the *Capricious*, is anchored in the bay. It's a sloop and it's easy to maneuver. I'll get a crew together later. All my men were hanged."

Benjamin was the first to climb up and put his head through the skylight.

"It's really high up," he exclaimed.

"Crouch on the outside windowsill and you'll be nearer the surface of the water. Then jump!"

The boy climbed out, took a deep breath, and toppled forward.

Plop! The sound of all three dives was masked by the continuous roar of surf on the shore.

Their heads bobbed to the surface. Moonlight cast a silver cloak over the sea. They could make out a dark shape against the sea, quite close to them. Was it a boat or a rock?

"Follow me!" ordered Mary.

A whirlwind of feathers swooped over them.

"The easterrrn cape, you rrrascals! Parrrabas awaits you!"

"Parabas?" repeated the young woman in amazement. "What's that rogue doing here?"

"He's come to get us," Louise said. "We set you free so you would get us out of the fort. Now we go

our separate ways."

Red Mary was still stunned but anger quickly took over and she lunged out to push the children's heads underwater, but the approach of a small boat stopped her.

"We'll meet again!" she hissed. "I have more surprises in store for you two!"

Then she plunged underwater and swam off to get out of sight of the pirates. Two crewmen helped the children clamber on board the boat. Just then there was a cannon shot. The sound rolled across the night sky like thunder.

"The jailer must have come round and sounded the alarm. If they catch us, it's the rope…" shivered Benjamin.

"Hee, hee, hee," laughed Scarface, one of the crew sent to rescue the youngsters. "Now you're real pirates!"

The *Angry Flea*, with its lights extinguished, lay nearby.

"Welcome aboarrrd!" Shut-your-trap! shrieked. "Haul up the moorrrings! Cast off the lines! Let's get going, son of a sharrrk!"

The ship turned slowly on its keel. Its sails caught the wind just as a trail of fire spilled out from the fort, lighting up the bay and the surrounding coastline.

"Good luck to you, Red Mary!" Louise shouted, raising her hand in a salute.

"Red Mary? Curses—so she's free now!" Parabas muttered, puffing on his pipe. "I'll need to be on my guard. I have a feeling that there might be quite a crowd in Les Cayes, all looking for Cap'n Roc."

He went back to join the children, who were leaning against the rail.

"Shut-your-trap! carried out his mission perfectly," he told them. "He found the ship near Hispaniola and let us know that you were in Port Royal. He's a very special bird."

"That's true," agreed Benjamin. "And yet there are times when it really would be better if he shut his trap…"

"Do you know Red Mary?" asked Louise.

"I've heard of her," Parabas admitted evasively,

"but I've never met her. Anyway, she's just like any other pirate except that she's a woman."

"Hmm, you don't sound very convincing," Louise said to herself. "Mary seemed to know you all right!"

Parabas laid a hand on each of their shoulders.

"Well now, my young friends, it's time you told me what happened after you ended up on the ghost ship when we were caught in the fog…"

"First, let's just breathe in some of this lovely fresh air for a while," replied Louise.

"Yes," Benjamin chimed in, "we've almost forgotten the smell of freedom!"

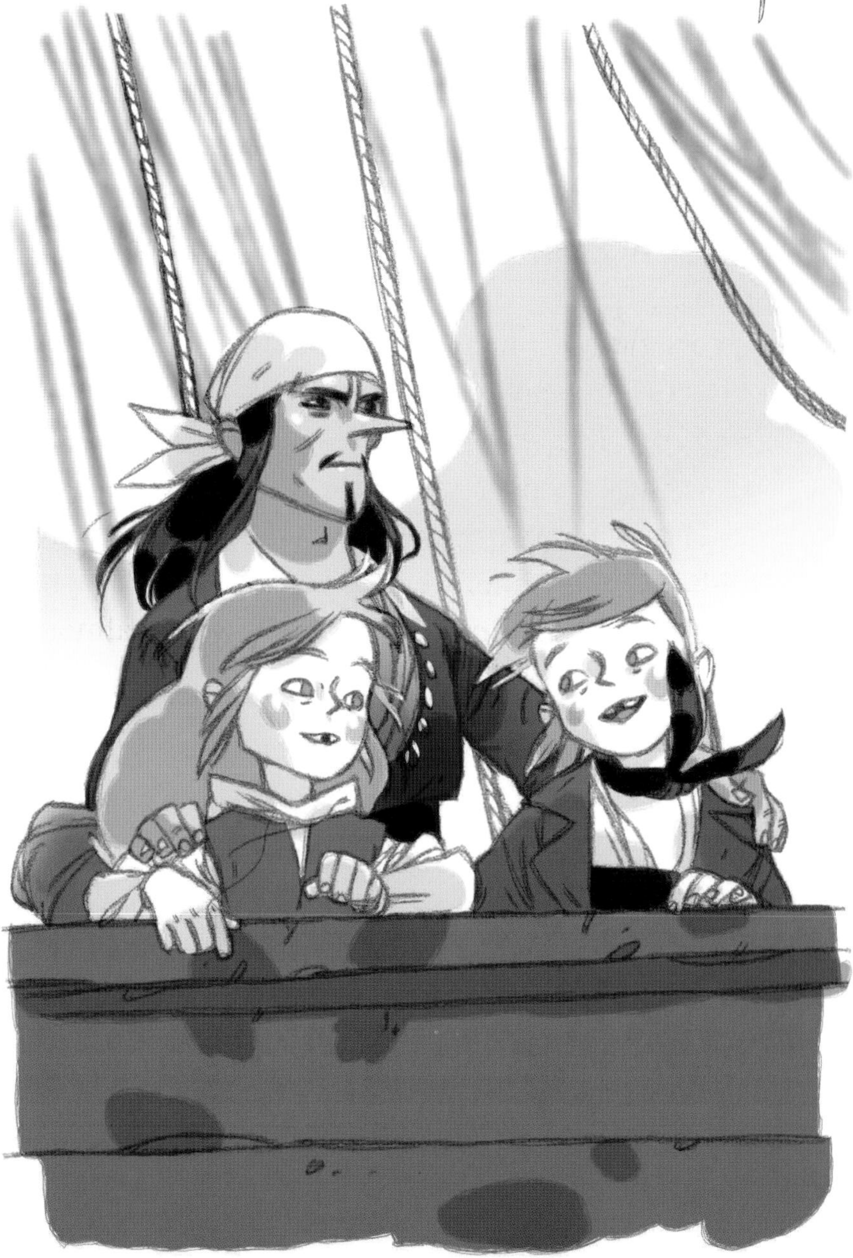

## ABOUT THE AUTHOR

Alain Surget is a professor of history as well as a prolific novelist. He started writing plays and poetry at the early age of 14, then went on to write more than 50 novels. Many of these are set in Ancient Egypt, or have animal conservation as their theme.

Alain is married with three children and lives in France. Despite writing about the sea in the Jolly Roger series of novels, he rarely sets foot in it, preferring life in the mountains.

## ABOUT THE ILLUSTRATOR

Annette Marnat loved drawing as a child, and went on to study illustration in Lyon, France, where she still lives. When she graduated in 2004, her work was selected for the Bologna Children's Book Fair Illustrators catalogue, and commissions from publishers soon followed. She is now a well-established and popular children's book illustrator.

# CONTENTS